A THUNDER CITY NOVELLA

A SECRET LOVE

DEBRA JESS

1

DURING THE GRAND finale of Blood Hunter

ALEK BLACKWOOD ANGLED his Rogue Pirate toward the dragon boss bearing down on his avatar. Maybe playing a round of *Battleguards of the Northern Kingdoms* wasn't such a good idea. The initial eruption of fire breath hit his avatar and the boom from his 3D sound bar jarred his memory, reminding him of the horrors he'd been facing.

The action on the screen faded and once again he hovered in mid-air. Alex watched from across the cargo container he had balanced on top of an air pillow as the jagged edge debris slammed into Evan — Rumble, his brother. Evan lost control of his side of the air pillow, sending the container slamming into Alek and breaking his leg. Alek ignored the crushing pain as Evan started to fall into the fire below, black smoke blooming upwards. From the boardwalk a flash of yellow surged forward into the inferno. Serena — Highlight — led the charge to save the Star Haven delegates directly underneath the massive container, not hesitating for a second to dive into danger to save the same people who would have been happy to see all alternative humans dead. Alek had a split second to make a choice: drop the container onto Serena and save his twin brother or hold the container and let Evan die.

Evan, half of Alek's soul, tumbled into the fiery hell below.

Alek dropped the controller and dug the heels of his hands into his eyes, but even the dance of color behind his eyelids didn't erase the choice he'd made. He'd been so careful, so very careful, for the past ten years to not make mistakes when Thunder City's Alt Support Services, T-CASS, called for a raid. This wasn't a mistake though; it was a choice. His choice. Who to save, and who to leave behind. He'd chosen Serena over his own brother. At some point, he'd have to tell them — both of them — but how?

Mandatory medical leave due to his broken left leg had given him way too much time to think about his choice. He'd spent the past two days procrastinating. He owed Thunder City's Alt Support Services an action report on the harbor raid. Instead he'd set up a VR system for his youngest brother, Cory, and Cory's girlfriend Hannah, to use to communicate while they were under investigation by the Oversight Committee. It was the least he could do after Hannah had healed his leg and Cory stopped him from tearing up the hospital in fit of grief.

The empty first page with the blinking cursor was still active on his desktop system, tucked away in the second bedroom of his apartment with the door closed so he wouldn't have to see it. Everyone who'd been on duty during the harbor attack would have to submit a report. Those same people — his colleagues, his friends, his family — would read it.

Fucking hell, everyone would know about his choice.

If anyone demanded a review, he'd have to submit to an inquiry and justify his actions. To Evan. To Serena. To himself.

Rule of thumb: never fall in love with your oldest brother's on-again, off-again fiancée. It had been a bad idea thirteen years ago, and it was a bad idea now. Except thirteen years ago, Nik and Serena were *the* high school sweethearts, and he was just the adorable middle school sidekick. He knew he was adorable because Serena had said so, but he'd never been adorable enough to lure her away from Nik

He was still adorable, and he was still in love with Serena, and Serena was now available thanks to Nik's brand-new girlfriend, Daniella Rose.

None of which had anything to do with his choice.

Bullshit.

Music blared from his phone, making him jump and interrupting that useless train of thought. On the TV screen, his avatar lay dead because of his inaction. For a second, Alek could have sworn the broken Rogue Pirate looked like Evan.

It's just your guilt and your imagination running wild.

He'd made his choice. He'd saved Serena instead of Evan. How was he supposed to live with that decision? He wasn't in the mood to talk but checked the phone just to see who was calling.

Evan. Alek yanked the phone out of its charging dock.

"You're not responding to your comm."

Evan's annoyance reassured Alek, calming his raw nerves. His brother was fine, but only because of his intense T-CASS training and the coordinated efforts of Pathia, T-CASS's telepath, and Hannah Quinn and Cory. Cory was the last brother Alek would have expected to stay by his side to force him to deal with Evan's near death. He'd been the one who had spoken for Pathia, who couldn't break through Alek's wall of pain to tell him Evan was alive.

"I just woke up." Alek sat up straighter and paused the game.

"We're on medical leave until Mom says otherwise. No one should be contacting us via the comm."

"There's been an attack on Harbor Regional Hospital." Alek could hear a television playing from Evan's end of the phone. "Thomas has been shot. Mom is down there with Nik. Someone's planted bombs around the hospital."

Alek stared at his dead avatar. In his mind's eye, the avatar's face changed to Thomas's. Thomas wasn't his favorite person in the world, but Alek had never wished him dead. Well, at least not since he'd grown past his teenage attitude. If his stepfather didn't survive, his mother would be devastated.

"I'll be ready in five. You can meet me at the corner of — "

"No way. We can't go down there. Mom's orders. Check your damn comm."

Alek grabbed the other device, scrolling through the half dozen voice-to-text messages organizing the response to this attack. Even though he knew Evan wouldn't lie about the orders, he looked for the private message sent to them by his mother.

Don't you two even think about it. Stay away. I'll contact you if I need you.

His mother knew them well. God only knew what she was going through, almost losing all four of her sons in the past few weeks, and now maybe losing her husband? Still, his mother had the strength of Atlas, both physically and emotionally. If she wanted them by her side, she would have said so.

He kept scrolling, looking for a message from Serena. That one wouldn't be private because why would it be? She had no idea how he felt about her, and that was for the best.

"All right. We won't go downtown, but we can still go to HQ." If T-CASS hadn't called in Serena, she would be above headquarters in the sports arena, training the Star Haven Newcomers. The Newcomers were Alts who had fled Star Haven after the Alt ban became the city's law. The Newcomers had to prove they could control their abilities before they would be allowed to live in Thunder City. It was Serena's responsibility to make it happen. No one dared doubt she couldn't do it, least of all, Alek.

"If you want," Evan said, "but use the roof entrance and don't wear your uniform. I think Mom's more worried about advertising that Hannah healed us than about our health."

The news media must have picked up footage of Evan's fall and his own broken leg. Hannah could heal with a simple touch, but the Oversight Committee wanted both her and Cory, who had translocation abilities, arrested. Both of them had ignored the Committee's orders to end their relationship until they could prove their control over their powers. The same Committee included Serena as a member. It was a mess.

"Will you meet me there?" he asked Evan, already guessing the answer.

"No. I'm going to the clinic. They're shorthanded as it is."

When they weren't saving Thunder City as Rumble and Roar, Evan worked at a veterinary hospital. Alek figured it was the best place for Evan to lie low until the legal situation with Hannah and Cory was handled.

"I'm heading to the clinic now," Evan said. "Text me if you learn anything new at HQ."

Alek could hear Evan slide the glass doors open to the porch outside his own apartment.

"Will do." As he looked around his own apartment, Alek disconnected. His mail had piled up over the past few weeks. Like Evan, he had a side hustle: he reviewed video games and computer equipment for several prominent industry magazines and was designing his own game for eventual release. His apartment had at least three layers of cardboard shipping boxes filled with all sorts of games and equipment from companies requesting reviews. He'd have to break it all down later.

Even without the rush of responding to the hospital emergency, it still only took Alek five minutes to wash up, change into clean jeans and a fresh t-shirt, and head for the roof of his apartment building. He had an agreement with the landlord to give him free access to the roof so that he could launch at a moment's notice. It was easier than jumping out the window. He'd tried that once. It hadn't ended well for the window.

He launched, using the power of the vortex he created to propel himself in the sky. With practiced ease, he scanned the airspace around him, expecting to see the usual: aerialists like himself or a low flying aircraft or two. Instead, the entire eastern sky, directly over downtown, lit up with the brightest firework he'd ever seen. Alek braked in mid-air, the explosion triggering his horror three seconds before the shock wave hit, knocking him off course. The wave was followed by a deafening boom.

Mom!

The nightmare looped again — the explosion, the debris hitting Evan, the container hitting his own leg, breaking it, Serena running underneath the cargo container.

Alek extended his Alt ability, pulling at the air in desperation, forcing himself into a controlled tumble until he could right himself. His flight back under control, Alek scanned the sky one more time.

It had to be his mother flying one of the bombs into the atmosphere. Only she would have the physical power to withstand an explosion of that magnitude. Thunder City called her Captain Spectacular for a reason: she was one of the strongest alternative humans alive. Coupled with her ability to fly, she had the physical strength of an army tank. She was damn near impossible to stop. Alek might have been able to fly the bomb into the atmosphere, but if he'd been closer to the explosion, it would have killed him.

He waited, hanging there, his ears ringing, his mind looping one more time, showing Evan falling into the cargo ship blast, Serena flying underneath him. He pulled out his comm, but there was no way he could hear a message. He'd have to text it, but his fingers stumbled over the keys. He took a deep breath to steady his fingers. As he did, the scent of sugar cookies sent a calming wave through him.

They're fine, Alek.

Pathia? You can talk to me now?

You're not angry, or combative, like you were two days ago. You want to hear me. Your mother is fine.

Instead of naming each of his family members, he rapidly pictured each one of them in his head. Pathia would understand without words. Evan. Nik. Cory. Hannah. Thomas. He added Serena at the end. He couldn't help it.

Evan was too far away, heading to the clinic. Nik and Cory are also fine. I cannot reach Hannah. I'm not able to read her, but I'm not as familiar with her thoughts as I am with you and your family. An ambulance is transporting Thomas to the Fargrounds Medical Center. I'll keep looking for Hannah, I promise.

Alek looked back in the direction of the hospital. Thunder City would have a real problem on their hands if Hannah died.

Go to the Arena, Alek. Go see Serena. She has her hands full and could use help.

The sweet scent disappeared. Did Pathia know about his choice? His crush?

Stupid question; of course she did. She would never say anything to anyone, though. He'd known her almost as long as he'd known Serena. Telepaths had their own code of ethics. If anyone could be trusted with a secret it was Pathia, but what did she mean by telling *him*, specifically, to see Serena? Was she encouraging him? Did she know if Serena had finally gotten over Nik and was ready for someone new?

Orders continued to ping on his comm. The debris from the explosion continued to rain, as other T-CASS aerialists launched around the hospital, protecting those on the ground. Alek's hands still shook; his ears still rang.

He clenched his fists tight as he increased the vortex of air keeping him still. Pathia had said that Serena needed him. Maybe this was his chance to get closer to her and show her he was more than Nik's younger brother. With a push, he headed toward headquarters once more, picking up speed. Evan might be fine, but the bombing at the hospital must have affected headquarters. Whatever had happened, he would be there to help Serena deal with it.

Once again, Alek chose Serena over his brother.

"KEEP WALKING, Grey. You can do this." Serena Jakes secured a gloved hand around Scott Grey's waist, as she guided him off the Arena's basketball court. Though he'd been born Cory Blackwood, he'd taken on the identity of Scott Grey when he was adopted by his stepfather.

All of the Blackwood men were big. After a decade and three broken engagements with Scott's oldest brother Nik, she would know better than most.

There was no time to think about Scott's brother or her broken heart. The cacophony of crying babies echoed through the Arena. Scott had saved all of them with his newly discovered translocation ability, but the cost was his exhaustion. She'd seen this before while training the Star Haven Newcomers. Overusing their alternative human ability before they could fully control it was like running a marathon before you had completed a 5k.

Alts wound up tiring themselves out to the point where they would need medical care to recover.

"Zach!" Serena called to one of her speedsters.

He appeared in front of her like magic. "Yes, ma'am!"

"Round up Josh, Yael, and Tessa. Go to every pharmacy between here and downtown. We're going to need diapers, formula, bottles, and wet wipes. Also, pick up food for the older kids. Fun snacks, but low on sugar. Tell the managers to bill T-CASS."

"Yes, ma'am."

Zach disappeared just as fast as he had appeared. It wouldn't be long before he would prove his control to the Oversight Committee and the public would vote on his moniker. She hoped it was something as fun as his personality.

In the meantime, Scott was getting heavier on her shoulders, so she had to keep moving toward the secured elevator that would take them to T-CASS headquarters. He needed fluids and proteins, but to get either she had to keep him upright. Had she mentioned how big Scott Grey was?

"Hold up, Serena. Let me give you a hand." Alek Blackwood exited the elevator she was aiming for.

"Gloves, Blackwood!" Some days she felt as if she were the only one who followed protocol around here. Regardless of Scott's accomplishment, he was still a trainee and couldn't be touched with bare hands. She never took hers off when she was around trainees specifically for this reason. You never knew when an accident could occur.

Scott was still breathing heavy by the time Alek returned with gloves on his hands.

She should have been relieved when Alek took the brunt of Scott's weight off her shoulders, except now she was surrounded by Blackwoods. At least it was Alek and not Nik. Where was Nik anyway?

It doesn't matter. Unless he's running an operation, he's not your problem anymore.

Since when did she ever think of Nik as a problem?

Since he jumped from your bed into Daniella Rose's.

"You shouldn't be here, Alek." She had to shout to make herself heard over the crying infants, and to drown out the voice in her head. "You're on medical leave."

"Yeah, which is why I'm here and not downtown evacuating the hospital."

Serena stopped short, eliciting a groan from Scott. "What happened this time?" She'd been training the Newcomers all afternoon but suspected something when T-CASS dispatchers patched Grey's call through to her.

"I'll tell you later. Let's get Cory below."

Alek was right. The situation in the Arena was under control. She needed to focus on getting Scott medical care. Serena noted that Alek still used his brother's birth name, instead of his adopted one. She used the name Scott had chosen for himself. Scott hadn't seemed to care one way or the other.

All three of them slumped against the back of the elevator as it descended. Neither Alek nor Scott looked at her, but she couldn't help her cursory examination of the brothers. Scott didn't like her much, but she was used to that. Most trainees didn't like her until they finished their training, though there were some who avoided her even after they'd graduated.

Well, let them hate on her all they wanted. She had a job to do, and there were rules for a reason. She and Alek worked together just fine for T-CASS operations. Unlike her trainees, Alek had known her since Nik had brought her home that first time to meet his folks. Of all of Nik's brothers, Alek was the one she liked the most because he respected her authority while others viewed her as pedantic.

Even though she'd struggled — and mostly failed — to maintain her relationship with Nik after graduation, Alek was always there in the background. They weren't exactly friends but were more than colleagues. They gamed together in the evenings, an activity in which Nik had no interest. Alek and Nik were close, though, so she had to be careful about what they talked about.

The elevator doors opened. Alek continued to keep Scott leaning on him while Serena ushered them through headquarters, an oval room with massive television screens embedded above, streaming the news from both sides of Mystic Bay. T-CASS dispatchers, called "worker bees" because of the yellow polo shirts they wore, either sat at their stations lining the walls or gathered in groups to consult with their colleagues. Serena could overhear the words "gunfire," "bombs," and "evacuate" as she reached the hallway leading toward the emergency medical unit.

Small injuries and minor illnesses could be handled by one of the nurses or medics on duty. Bigger injuries would get transferred to the hospital's alternative medicine clinic...if there was still a clinic to be transferred to. What the hell had happened?

"Status?" One of the nurses approached, already pulling on blue disposable gloves.

"Fatigue and possible dehydration," Serena said. She had no medical training, but she'd seen this many times before.

"What's his ability?"

"Translocation."

"Has he finished his training?"

"No," she confirmed.

"Cory, do you need anything?" Alek asked, his voice oddly gentle for a guy who hadn't had anything nice to say about his youngest brother in over a decade.

"Hannah." Serena barely heard Scott's whispered response. "I don't know where she is. The Shield won't tell me."

Serena's annoyance rose. Who the hell was Shield? She knew the names and monikers for every alternative human in the T-CASS database. No one used "Shield."

"If I see her, I'll send her right to you. Do as the nurse says and rest." Alek laid a hand on his brother's shoulder.

Scott's eyes closed and Alek backed away to let the nurse do her thing.

"Alek, join me, please." Serena made her way out of medical, down another hallway to her own office. She touched her thumb to the keypad lock on the door, then motioned Alek inside first.

He slumped into the guest chair as she pulled out her own from behind the desk to join him.

"Obviously, you know something I don't. What happened at the hospital? Why do we have an Arena filled with children? And who the hell is Shield?"

Alek scrubbed his face, a cute habit he had when he was tired or overwhelmed. It had been some time since she'd seen him like this, but between the quarry raid last week and the harbor attack three days ago, she didn't blame him for his exhaustion. Almost losing his twin to a terrorist attack had to be a special kind of nightmare.

"Someone shot Thomas."

No! Thomas Carraro, Hack-Man, ran the operations side of T-CASS, and he was damn good at it. Serena respected him but had avoided him in the HQ hallways ever since her last hook-up and break-up with Nik.

"Who shot him? Why? Where was he when it happened?"

"I don't know who shot him or why, but it happened at Harbor Regional. All I know is what I'm getting over the comm. Terrorists planted bombs all around the building. Nik, Jack, and

Gavin disarmed most of them, but Mom had to fly one into the atmosphere before it exploded. We don't know where Hannah is. I don't know who Shield is."

Serena grabbed her personal phone and sent an auto message to her mother, who worked at a bank downtown, to confirm that she was okay. If she didn't get a response, she'd alert someone. She'd sent that same message enough times in her life that she didn't even have to take her eyes off of Alek to do it.

It didn't take a genius to figure out that Hannah had healed Alek's broken leg, so she had to be somewhere accessible. Serena would bet Hannah also healed Evan as well, both illegal acts since Hannah hadn't proven her control yet. Both she and Scott had challenged the Oversight Committee and lost. She knew because she had voted to have them arrested. Alek would know that too if he ever got around to reading the report, but there was no reason to mention it now, not when he sat there looking so miserable.

"Do you want me to check on Thomas's status?"

Alek shook his head. "Thomas is alive but had to be transferred to the Fargrounds Medical Center. Pathia let me know. That's the last I heard."

"Then Thomas will be fine." She reached out to take his gloved hands into hers. Not the best way to make a personal connection, but it would have to do. "Fargrounds Medical is just as good as Harbor Regional, probably better because they get more gunshot victims. They'll take good care of Thomas, I'm sure."

"I know." Alek closed his fingers around her hands, his head bowed so he wasn't looking at her. She wouldn't force him to look up if he didn't want to. His voice was almost too quiet for her to hear.

"Is there anything I can do?" she asked. "Anything else I should know?"

Alek shook his head but looked at her this time. "If Mom —
the Captain — wanted you downtown, she would have let you
know. Right now, there's nothing we can do but wait."

"Wait and speculate." Serena couldn't help putting pieces of
the puzzle together. "This attack — it's just like Miranda Dane at
the quarry."

"Yeah, but right under our noses this time."

"And using children. Babies." She enjoyed working with little
kids, had loved holding her neighbor's newborn in her arms the
last time they'd invited her over. How could anyone hurt a child?
"And Hannah's in the middle of all of this?"

"It's not her fault." Alek pulled his hand out of hers to rub the
back of his neck. "It's not Cory's, either. It's no one's fault but the
anti-Alt groups."

Serena had her doubts about Hannah but couldn't blame
Alek for defending the Blood Surfer. Everyone wanted Hannah
to continue to do what she'd been doing: healing people without
impediment.

Except Serena had sat on the Committee for both Scott and
Hannah's cases. The quarry raid, the harbor attack, and now the
hospital bombing...all of these had occurred after Hannah
arrived in Thunder City. She might not be responsible, but her
mother had been the mayor of Star Haven and Hannah's
presence here had her set off the chain reaction. "Maybe. Where
is she now? And who is this Shield? What is his connection to
Scott?"

"Like Cory said, we don't know where Hannah is, and I have
no idea who the Shield is or how he knows Cory."

Before she could press Alek further, her own comm
chimed.

"What does it say?" Alek asked.

"We're all on stand down for the for next seventy-two hours."
She couldn't believe the orders, even though the words were

clear. "All of us. The entirety of T-CASS. Captain Spec is calling in the reserve team."

"I guess you're done for the day."

Serena reread the order. "But...I can't just leave. What about all of the infants upstairs? What about the Star Haven Newcomers? There will be an investigation. I should be here to answer any questions."

"How can you answer questions when you don't have any of the answers? None of us do." Alek pulled off his gloves, which was fine as they'd proven their control a long time ago, and the ugly brown things got hot and itchy after a while.

Serena discarded her own gloves as she wheeled her chair back behind her desk. "I can't sit here doing nothing."

"Serena, the Captain gave you a direct order to stand down for seventy-two hours. I can play fast and loose with Mom's orders, but you won't. You can't. It's not your style." He hesitated. "Why don't you come back to my place? I have food and drinks in the fridge. We can monitor things from there."

Serena considered his offer. Orders were orders, and if the Captain found her in her office when she was supposed to be on stand down, it wouldn't look good for her. She had ambition beyond being a training coordinator and a team leader, and she made no bones about wanting to join Captain Spec's inner circle, even if it meant being surrounded by Blackwoods. Even if it meant seeing Nik and Daniella every single damn day. It would hurt, but she'd cope. She wasn't about to let her personal life interfere with her professional life.

That was what she had never understood about the Blackwood brothers: Alek, Evan, Nik...they all had side jobs because they wanted to. Hell, even Scott had left Thunder City to become a cop in a city hostile to Alts.

T-CASS was her life. She'd dedicated herself to this organization because it was important. Not just for Alts, but for the Norms who shared Thunder City with them. It gave her life purpose and meaning, especially since she had no one else except her mother.

What about Tavia?

Serena squelched that thought. Her half-sister, Octavia, hadn't spoken to her for four years. Tavia had only ever called Serena when she needed her big sister to dig her out of trouble, which was often. Even then, Tavia would only contact her because Serena was an Alt, and Tavia wasn't.

Since her sister hadn't called, Serena had to assume Tavia was just fine. Believing otherwise made her sick to her stomach, and she couldn't live like that — always wondering if she should have done more to keep Tavia in her life.

Serena pushed Tavia to the back of her mind, so she could consider Alek's offer without that distraction. Alek had his own personal arsenal of computer equipment at home. He could, no doubt, get them the answers they didn't have with just a few clicks on a keyboard. All she had in her apartment was a mountain of laundry. "Fine, but I want to return to the basketball court first."

Alek stood and offered her his now bare hand to pull her out of her chair. She didn't mind a little chivalry once in a while.

If she couldn't have Nik, then she'd bury herself in her work. If she couldn't have love, then she would at least have respect. Alek respected her and T-CASS was her family, even if they didn't always appreciate her. That was just the way families were, and if she didn't want to become a hermit, she'd have to learn to live with it.

OCTAVIA JAKES FELT the panic bubble up from the depths of her soul. Her breath quickened as she fought the urge to run screaming from the converted stockroom where she sat for upwards of eight to ten hours a day, hunched over her computer, her fingers pounding on the keyboard while she manipulated her Demon Paladin. The job had become so easy over the years, and she'd become so good at what she did, that her boss didn't have to stand over her shoulder anymore. She had a little more freedom than she used to have, freedom that allowed her to multi-task — like watching the streaming news service in the corner of her screen while she played the game.

Are you still there?

Octavia glanced back to the chat box. The kid she'd been talking to was waiting for her response.

Sorry. Phone call.
Think about what I said.
We'd love for you to join us.

She looked at the steaming news again. The newscaster pointed toward Harbor Regional Hospital where a flurry of color zipped around the building. The colors were the uniforms worn by T-CASS, the alternative humans who were putting their lives on the line while evacuating the hospital. No one knew why the hospital needed evacuating, so the news cameras focused on the rescue efforts, showcasing Thunder City's heroes doing what they did best.

I'd like to, but my parents...
I don't have a driver's license yet.

Octavia had said the same thing before her boss had first recruited her. The answer was so easy, and simple, and true.

I'll send you my spare bus pass.
This is totally the club for you.
Everyone here is just like you.

The video stream changed tack and replayed the events of a few days ago. On screen Captain Spectacular dove below a massive cargo ship docked in the harbor, holding it above the water line, while the rest of T-CASS rescued the crew and the delegates from Star Haven.

One particular T-CASS member stood out to Octavia — the bright yellow uniform worn by Highlight, her sister. Octavia watched while Serena Jakes flew her light slide under the cargo container held in mid-air as if by magic, in order to rescue the Star Haven delegates underneath it. Of course, Serena would be in the thick of things, taking charge, acting like the hero Thunder City thought she was.

Octavia's fingers tensed on the keyboard, shaking. She watched Serena emerge with at least half of the delegates holding onto her as she guided her light slide away from the ship to safety.

The video skipped ahead thirty minutes to show the Captain emerging from the water, brushing herself off as if saving the city from devastation was just another day on the job for her. It *was* just another day saving Thunder City. The news didn't show what had happened to Serena, but that wasn't a surprise. Serena might be a hero, but she wasn't a member of the Blackwood family, no matter how hard she tried to be.

Did you see the news? Captain Spec
is saving Thunder City again.

Octavia jerked back to the chat box. She was losing her target, damn it. Her boss, Mister Kolar, was farther down the row talking to another club member working on one of the console games. She had time to pull the kid back into her world.

Captain Spec owns most of Thunder City.
Between her, Hack-Man, and her kids,
they control everything this side of Mystic Bay.

They're just protecting their assets.

No immediate response, so Octavia kept her eye on the news. *You mean we're all slaves to the Alts here? That's what they say in Star Haven.*

Octavia knew she should turn off the news and focus. She only needed to apply just a few more breadcrumbs to finish the job and report yet another successful invitation to Mister Kolar.

Yes. Star Haven has the right idea but they lack leadership. They use hammers, when they need paint brushes.

Another long pause while the kid typed out their answer. While Octavia waited, she listened to the newscaster gush about how efficient T-CASS was at handling the situation.

A second reporter broke into the story and the view changed from the harbor back to the hospital. Captain Spectacular crashed through the roof, sending debris flying across the helipad. Over her head, she carried a massive metal something. She flew so fast the cameraman couldn't keep up as she disappeared into a soft white cloud far above. A second later, the cloud lit up from the inside. The sharp light glowed for an instant, then darkened. The cloud returned to normal. Another few seconds passed, and Octavia heard the explosion. Her chair rattled with the force.

Did you feel that?

How the hell could she compete with Captain Spectacular?

Yeah, I felt it.

Do you think it was the Star Haven
anti-Alts who set the bomb?

> *Probably. Just remember what I said*
> *about hammers and paint brushes.*
> *The Star Haven anti-Alts are unsophisticated.*
> *They're going to lose the war for us*
> *if we don't do something. We're different.*
> *We'll use our brains, not our bombs*
> *to drive Alts out of our city.*

That was the core of the club's mission statement. Brains, not brawn; slow and steady. Ridding Thunder City of Alts would be a marathon, not a sprint. The words had been drilled into her by Mister Kolar. She could recite the entire script in her sleep.

Screams could still be heard from the news stream. Above it all, the reporter yelled that the hospital was empty and secure.

No lives had been lost during the earlier harbor rescue, either, but at least a couple of Captain Spectacular's sons — the twins, Rumble and Roar — had been wounded, knocking them off the playing field for a while. Thunder City would have to live without the two most popular Blackwood sons.

I can't tell my parents
about the party. They think
Alts can do no wrong. They
wish I were an Alt.

Octavia gritted her teeth. It wasn't unusual for kids to wish for an Alt ability, at least not in Thunder City where there were so damn many Alts. Parents who wanted their kids to become Alts made up another whole level of crazy Social Services had to deal with far too often. She would know about *that* better than most.

*What you see on TV isn't
the real story. Most Alts
aren't anything special.*

The news stream shifted again, speculating as to whether or not Star Haven would reconsider its controversial ban now that their top leadership had been rescued by Alts. Octavia knew better. The city that sat across Mystic Bay from Thunder City had the right idea by kicking out anyone with superhuman abilities.

*I mean imagine, if your Alt ability was
generating smoke from your fingertips.
Soft wisps of smoke. Nothing more.*

She didn't push for an answer right away. Folks needed to think this stuff through and come to their own conclusions.
*I guess it would be
pretty useless.*
Good. She had their attention back on her, not on the news.

*Exactly. Useless.
You couldn't join T-CASS
because you're no good in
a fight or rescuing people.*

Octavia ran her Demon Paladin avatar toward the edge of the animated bonfire on the screen. The kid's Mage Princess hovered along the edge of the crowd. She needed to make sure they were drawn into the larger conversation happening in the main chat room.

The news channels are just

looking to make money off the
Alts with flashy powers. Most
Alts have worthless abilities
and are a drain on society because
their powers make them crazy.

Next to Harbor Regional was the clinic set up just for alternative humans. Octavia figured the clinic must have been the real target, but the anti-Alt terrorists had planted their bombs around the wrong building. The clinic sucked up land that could have been used to expand the regular hospital, but instead it supported people who never should have existed in the first place, as Mister Kolar would say.

The party starts at 6:00 p.m.
right here at Cybervid Games.
Nothing big, just a group of us
playing Battleguards of the
Northern Kingdoms.

The news switched to interviewing patients who had been transferred to a different hospital. They all bragged about how the Alts had organized everyone, how safe they felt, how grateful they were.

Octavia looked at a picture tacked up on the cork board behind her computer. The picture showed Mister Kolar shaking hands with Miranda Dane, the mayor of Star Haven. No, the *former* mayor of Star Haven. Former because one of Captain Spec's sons had shot her when she got caught imprisoning Alts and experimenting on them.

Okay, but will
there be alcohol?

A shadow darkened Octavia's view of the screen. Mister

Kolar stood there, checking to make sure Octavia was doing what she was supposed to. His spiky black hair was meant to give his dad bod a younger, hipper look. No one wanted to hurt his feelings by telling him it didn't work.

No alcohol. Mister Kolar
is firm on that.
Snacks and soda only.

Lemonade? I'm not
supposed to drink soda.

Octavia looked up at Mister Kolar, whose lips twisted in a half-smile. That half-smile could charm a girl right out of her own family and into his.

A part of Octavia still wanted to do whatever she could to earn that smile.

"Tell them sure."

I'll make sure there's
some lemonade for you.

Okay, I'll be there if you
send the bus pass. Thanks.

Mister Kolar watched with Octavia as the Mage Princess ran forward into the crowd gathered around the town square's bonfire. What the kid didn't know was that the entire guild was made up of store employees, people like Octavia who sat around the stock room of Cybervid Games doing exactly what she was doing: recruiting.

"Good job. That's four we've added to the roster for Friday night."

"Yeah." Octavia tried to put some of the enthusiasm she used to feel into her voice — honest enthusiasm she had felt before two weeks ago. "It's getting harder, though, with all of the..." She paused because she'd almost said *heroics,* but that would just push Mister Kolar into lecture mode. The last thing she needed right now was an anti-Alt lecture. "...raids."

Mister Kolar huffed. "Hang in there and keep doing what you're doing. I still have contacts in Star Haven. The anti-Alt gangs over there are not helping us here. They're aggressiveness is hindering our cause. If Norms start dying in their attacks, we'll lose more employees than we'll gain."

"What do you mean?"

"I mean, if we're ever going destroy the Alts, we need more support for non-violent actions. We've succeeded in purifying Star Haven, but we did it by enacting anti-Alt laws, without risking the lives of Norms. If we're going to conquer Thunder City, we'll need more active soldiers, but we *have* to limit our targets to just Alts. Whoever advised this particular cell to blow up the hospital didn't consider the fact that every soldier we lose to the prison system, or to violent attacks like this fiasco, is one less soldier we have to finish the fight."

Octavia looked beyond the row of computers and console setups toward the cash register. A tip jar sat there, collecting for the families of the anti-Alt soldiers who had died fighting for the rights of Norms — normal humans without Alt abilities. She'd paid ten percent of her paycheck into the jar every week. No one forced her; she had wanted to do it.

Mister Kolar clapped a hand on her shoulder. "Stay at the bonfire. Engage with the recruits. Find out who their friends are and ask them to pass along the invitation for Friday night. Oh, and can you make that chocolate cake you made for the last party?"

Octavia's emotions squirreled around her gut. Mister Kolar liked her baking.

She loved to bake. No one else had ever asked her to bake for them until she met Mister Kolar and attended her first Cybervid Games party. "Sure thing. I'll make two since we're double the size that we were four months ago."

"Good job."

Mister Kolar moved down the row, encouraging the others, reviewing their chats, making sure things proceeded smoothly. Octavia looked down at her hands.

Smoke rose unbidden from the tips of her fingers.

2

ALEK RELEASED Serena's hand as soon as he pulled her to her feet. As much as he wanted to keep her hand in his, he didn't know how Serena would react if she got a hint of his interest in her. He didn't want to break the connection he'd just made. When she had taken his hands into hers, he couldn't risk looking at her and giving away his desire, an emotion inappropriate for the moment.

He said nothing as he followed her onto the elevator bringing them back up to ground level. Serena had always respected his desire to not talk when he just didn't feel like it. Oh, he could make small talk if he had to. He'd learned a long time ago that as a Blackwood, you were expected to say something polite, especially when a reporter stuck a microphone in your face. With Serena, he didn't feel the pressure to be witty when deep down, he just wanted to keep his thoughts to himself.

The silence of the elevator shattered as soon as the doors opened. Controlled chaos surrounded them. Boxes of diapers and formula had been stacked neatly along the bleachers. Star Haven Newcomers distributed blankets to the Thunder City

Tornadoes basketball team, who had arrived for their own practice session. Everyone with free hands cradled a baby or played with a toddler.

Zach appeared before them. "We got all of the supplies. I ran into a couple of Norm parents at the pharmacy. One called Social Services and explained the situation. The other called her babysitter and asked him to start a phone tree to get as many sitters down here as possible. We'll have help within the hour. They also said we would need pacifiers, changing mats, and sippy cups, so I got those too."

"Great job. I should have thought of those things myself."

Alek could see the young man swell with pride under Serena's praise. Handing out praise wasn't something Serena did often, but when she did, she meant it and she made sure her trainees knew it.

Serena kept talking to the boy. "I've been ordered to stand down for the next seventy-two hours. Do you think you can keep things under control until Social Services arrives?"

"Yes, ma'am."

The kid looked like he might salute Serena, but he marched back into the thick of things instead. Alek forced himself not to laugh. He would have saluted Serena himself if he thought for one second she would see him as a man and not just Nik's younger brother.

"C'mon." He nudged Serena. "Let me fly you back to my place. You've been working around the clock since before the quarry raid. It'll be less obvious than your light slide."

Outside in the parking lot, the mid-afternoon sun warmed up the late summer's day.

"Ready?"

He expected Serena to pull her arm away from him, but instead, she stepped closer. Had he ever carried her before? He couldn't remember having transported her during training or an operation. She must have seen him lift others, though, so she would have known that standing toe-to-toe wasn't necessary. Not that he minded; he was just surprised.

"Yes, I'm ready."

Instead of launching full tilt, as he would if he were flying alone, he started slow, with a swirl of air around their ankles. As his vortex built up pressure, he leaned into the gust. Serena followed his lead, her shoulder rubbing his arm. He focused his power underneath her. The farther she leaned, the stronger he created the vortex of wind swirling around them. He waited another few seconds for the pressure to build, then *swoop*, he lifted them into the air. Her hair, black and thick, pinned back only by a yellow feathered clip that matched her uniform, waved in the breeze. He loved to watch her hair, but he had to be careful to keep an eye out for other T-CASS aerialists who might have launched from the roof, eager to obey his mother's orders. The Arena faded as he gained altitude.

Serena continued to hold onto him, even though it wasn't necessary. He couldn't help but wonder what else she was thinking about. He banked again, heading toward the university district.

He landed with a gentle drop on the roof of his complex. Serena released his arm, the dissipating breeze cooling the bicep she had clung to. For a moment he was tempted to put her hand right back where it belonged, but his comm chimed. He had to check it in case it was another emergency.

"Are you okay?" Even though she had let him go, Serena stayed close. "Is it about Thomas?"

Alek realized that he must have frowned or something to clue in Serena about the message. "Yes, but good news. He's out of surgery. They're taking him to recovery."

"That's quick. I'm glad he'll be okay."

Alek put his comm away. "Mom says the bullet didn't hit any

bone, just flesh and muscle along the shoulder. She'll take him home as soon as he wakes up "

"Good." She frowned, and placed her hand back on his arm, the warmth that he'd missed returning. "You don't have to fake concern for me, Alek. I know about your feelings for your stepfather."

"Do you?" He snapped before he could stop himself. What the hell was he doing? He'd dreamed of spending time alone with Serena, and now that he had a chance to do it, Thomas was going to screw up things.

No, that was the excuse of a teenager. He was just starting to patch things up with Cory, which meant getting over his juvenile dislike of Thomas.

"Sorry, I didn't mean to snap, and I don't want you to think that I wish harm to Thomas. Some people just rub me the wrong way and he's one of them. As much I would have preferred Mom marrying someone else, Thomas is here to stay. I'll deal."

Serena nodded, sympathy softening her features as some of her hair escaped its clip and blew into her face. Alek held up his other hand, using his control over the air to redirect the wind. With little more than a thought, he forced the breeze to curve around Serena's body, allowing her hair to settle into a sexy, tousled look.

"Thanks." Serena readjusted the yellow clip, maybe to reassure herself that it was still in place. Alek wished she would remove it.

Imagining Serena with her hair down wouldn't cool his desire to run his fingers through the dark strands, so he looked away. He needed to find his control, or he might lose this chance to impress her. "Let's head inside. I think we're both tired. Maybe this seventy-two-hour stand-down isn't such a bad idea."

Alek led her down a set of stairs to his floor. He disengaged the security lock to his apartment a half second before he remembered the nightmare he'd left behind. Cardboard boxes — some empty, some still taped closed — covered almost every flat surface in the living room.

"Let me guess, you collect boxes for your brother's cats to sit in?"

Alek knew she was joking, but his stomach sunk with disappointment. How could he impress her with this mess? When he thought back to what he'd seen in her office—not a single paper or pen out of place — he couldn't imagine that Serena would invite him back to her apartment unless she knew it was pristine. Not that she had a reason to invite him in the first place — yet. Nothing to do about it now.

"I'm sorry about this." Once again, he used his control over the air. One by one he lifted the empty boxes off the floor, crushing them for the recycle bin.

"No, it's fine." Serena headed toward the sofa, stepping lightly over a box of cables. She scooped up the remote and chose a news channel. "Really. You should see the pile of laundry I have in my washroom. I get it. The raids haven't given us a lot of time at home."

Hearing her confess to not having time to do her laundry eased his embarrassment somewhat. "Let me clear a path to the kitchen. You can at least get yourself something to drink while I move the rest of these boxes into my office."

"I have a better idea." Alek watched her created a slide, a much smaller one than what she used outside. She hopped onto the flat, stable surface of pure light she'd pulled from his lamps and windows. Thank heavens, his apartment also had high ceilings. Few people, even non-T-CASS Alts, understood how much control you needed over your Alt ability to pull off such a simple maneuver. He knew, though, and his heart beat a little faster as he watched her glide over the mess with expert precision.

Once she reached the refrigerator, she dissipated the slide. Alek forced himself to concentrate on the boxes, rather than on Serena's graceful figure. He created a conveyor belt of wind, carrying the boxes into his office in a steady stream. By the time Serena reappeared, back on her slide, he could see the carpet again.

"Since we're not on duty...." She wiggled a couple of bottles of hard cider in her hands.

"Should hit the spot." He motioned for Serena to sit next to him on the sofa while he opened the bottles with a quick twist of his wrist.

She jumped off the slide with same practiced ease as before, the slide fading without a sound. They sat and watched the news for a few minutes. Most of what they saw was a replay from a couple of hours ago. Jack, Mach Ten, was the most obvious in his Day-Glo green uniform, zipping from one bomb to the next and disarming them faster than anyone could see. Nik then appeared, popping up through the concrete to get to the harder to reach bombs.

Serena tensed beside him, her posture becoming more rigid, her jaw tightening. Alek should have known his oldest brother would be in the middle of the mess. He'd learned to disarm bombs a couple of years ago, accepting a challenge from Blockhead, a former Marine, who could smash concrete when he shifted his hands into huge blocks. No one ever figured Nik would need to put that sort of education to practical use.

Alek reached for the remote. "Let's switch the channel."

"No. It doesn't matter." Serena brushed his hand away, shrugging her shoulders, but Alek knew better. The way she lifted her chin just a thread higher than necessary spoke louder than words. Seeing Nik, even on screen, hurt. "All the channels will be showing the same footage, more or less. Regardless of our break-up, I'll still have to work with him."

The scene changed. Instead of Nik, it showed Captain Spectacular flying a bomb larger than herself up into the clouds where it lit up the sky, concluding the dramatic news cycle. Alek was used to seeing his mother fly into danger, so watching her grab a bomb big enough to wipe out a couple of square city blocks didn't bother him at all.

Before the news cycle started again, a reporter appeared, managing to corner Nik before he could leave the scene. The reporter asked about Thomas. Nik said he didn't know but asked the public for their thoughts and prayers. Beside Nik, a huge hulk of a man appeared.

Serena inhaled, her shock matching Alek's. Neither of them had seen Daniella Rose shift into Daniel, or even her other alter ego, Dodger. This had to be Dodger, and mother-of-God was he huge. Dodger dwarfed Nik, who was the same height and weight as his brothers. The only resemblance Alek could see between Daniella, who barely reached five feet tall, and Dodger was the man bun holding back light brown wavy hair and fierce lavender eyes.

"Well, he's certainly impressive."

Alek could sense Serena sinking deeper into the sofa cushions, her posture collapsing as if crushed under the weight of her thoughts. Her body language screamed *outclassed*. To see Serena fading like that broke his heart too. Without thinking, he scooped up the remote and found a no signal channel.

"What are you doing?" Serena sat up straighter.

"You don't need to see Daniel, or Daniella, or whoever they are today. You can deal with them another day. Right now, we're on leave and as long as Thomas is alive, and no one else got hurt, we don't need to watch the news any further." He leaned down to pull his gaming console out from under the coffee table.

She watched him hook up the console. "Gaming? You want to play games now?"

"Do you have anything better to do?" He stretched so he could reach all of the cables connecting the console to the TV, making sure each one was secure. With all the wind he'd created crushing boxes, he might have jarred one loose.

"I guess not." Her voice, quieter and more unsure than he ever heard before, hardened his resolve.

With the flick of a switch, he populated the screen with icons for two dozen or so games: some he owned outright, others he was reviewing. He clicked on a colorful icon in the upper right corner. Before the game even started, Serena entire posture changed again, losing its hard edge, loosening into excitement.

"Alek, tell me that wasn't..."

The splash screen appeared, with the title *Battleguards of the Northern Kingdoms*. He looked over at Serena, her eyes wide with excitement.

"I thought they'd shut down this game forever. You know I love *Battleguards*. When did this happen?"

Alek could see her fingers twitch, wanting to grab the controls out of his hands. Yes, he knew how much she loved this game. They'd been members of the same guild for over a decade before the game company went under, burying the game too. They'd mourned the loss of their avatars over a late-night chat room in another game.

"You've been busy training the Newcomers and I do this for a living. I get free stuff all the time to review with advance purchase options. I'll text you the purchase code, so you can download it at home. I haven't had a chance to read up on the details, but the IP owners sold their rights to a new company. Not only did they reboot the game, with a few added modifications, but the original gamers were allowed to port their characters over from the old IP servers. I, uh, took the liberty of porting over your avatars along with mine. I hope you don't mind?"

"Oh, this is better than all my birthdays put together." Serena snatched a second controller off the floor, her fingers already manipulating the trackball.

At least she wasn't thinking about Nik or Daniella. The pure joy radiating from her face while she reactivated her avatar made his insides melt. Instinct forced him to clamp down on his Alt ability as the air around him stirred just enough to ruffle the hair on his arms. Classic goob mistake: letting his emotions control his power. If he couldn't keep control, especially in front of Serena, there would be repercussions of the personal and professional kind.

"We've got seventy-two hours and a fridge full of cider and snacks. What do you say?"

She didn't say anything; she didn't have to. In a second, they were both in the game, running their avatars around a familiar, yet slightly altered city.

"The graphics are so much better," Serena said, sounding more like the Serena he loved. "Sharper. The colors really pop and the details...I feel like I'm back home."

"Given all the time we spent playing when we were kids, it shouldn't be a surprise that it feels like home."

Now she looked at him. "*You* were the kid. *I* was an adult." With that pronouncement, she deliberately turned her nose up in the air in an affected attitude. Just the curve of her neck extending from her shoulders, and the dark skin she exposed from the seam of her uniform, distracted him from the mock argument she was leading him into.

"You were still in high school," he managed to stutter, but still couldn't tear himself away from her perfect profile. "We were both kids, at least as far as Mom and Dad were concerned."

She laughed. "I guess you're right, from that perspective. At least your dad took time off to meet me that first time."

His parents had been divorced for years, and Cory's father hadn't lived long enough to meet Serena or anyone else. His mother dated occasionally over the next decade, but it wasn't until Thomas rescued Cory that his mother found a husband who satisfied her. Thinking about his stepfathers wasn't helping his strategy, not with Serena sitting next to him, as desirable and comfortable as he could have imagined. He watched her hands manipulate the controls, guiding her avatar across the screen. "Look, you even have in-game mail already."

"Probably an admin notice," she said, but angled her avatar toward the mailbox in front of the city's town hall.

He woke up his Rogue Pirate and followed her Spirit Hunter but collected his own mail so it wouldn't look as if he were reading her messages over her shoulder. His inbox was filled with exactly what she'd predicted: admin notices, guild invites, nothing interesting.

"Oh, no. Tavia, what have you done?"

Alek closed his mailbox. Whatever was in Serena's inbox had erased her contented look and replaced it with the anguish. "What is it?"

"My sister. She's in the game too. Look at what she sent me."

This gave him the perfect excuse to scoot closer to Serena, the warmth of his body sending all the wrong signals at the wrong time. He read the message on the screen.

Help me.

IF SHE HADN'T HAD the gaming console in her lap, Serena would have stood up and stomped across the room. As it was, she pounded her left fist into the sofa cushion, an inappropriate response given that it wasn't her sofa. It wasn't even her apartment.

"I have to go." She picked up the controls to hand back to Alek, but found his hands cradling hers before she could free herself. It was a mirror image of her holding his hands back in her office, except this time she could feel his rough skin against her own.

"You just got here. Slow down a minute."

Serena hesitated. Tavia's message said *help me.* The heartache her sister had inflicted with each cry for help over the years crawled over Serena's heart. At least the grief gave her space between her own pain and Alek's concern. What the hell had she been thinking, coming to his apartment? She should have gone straight home and done her laundry and the half-dozen other chores that needed to get done. Seventy-two hours wouldn't last forever.

If you had gone home, you'd never have known your sister was in trouble.

The ripping open of long scabbed over wounds slowed. She put the console back in her lap, for lack of any other place to put it. Alek's hands stayed wrapped around hers, caught between the console and her legs, and for the first time she noticed how much bigger Alek's hands were than her own.

The last time she had held his hand, he'd been thirteen, when Nik had brought her home to meet his family. It took all of her stubbornness to not lose her courage in the face of meeting Nik's — and Alek's — parents, the legendary Captain Spectacular and Spook. Nik had told her it would also be Alek and Evan's thirteenth birthday party, so she'd quizzed Nik on what the boys' hobbies were. She'd spent hours picking out what she'd hoped would be the perfect birthday gifts. The last thing she wanted was for her heroes to think she had no social graces at all and turn up at the party empty-handed.

For Alek, she chose *Battleguards of the Northern Kingdoms,* the hot new game of the season, hoping his parents hadn't already bought it for him. Watching him rip open the wrapping paper, while everyone else was cooing over the passes to the Thunder City Zoo she'd bought for Evan, she could see his excitement build until the cover was revealed. He had declared, "I'm going to play this *now.*" Then he had grabbed her hand and off they went. Nik found her two hours later, tucked away with Alek in the video room, after all the birthday cake had been eaten. Nik had never liked games, only tolerating them to please her, but his heart was never in it.

Intellectually, she knew Alek's hands would have grown along with the rest of him, but it was still a bit of a shock. She'd watched Alek grow up. They were at most friendly colleagues. So, why was she just now taking note of the strength flowing from his firm grip? Even when she'd held onto him while he flew her here, she hadn't given his size or his strength a second thought. All she had wanted to do was offer the comfort of her presence, given the situation with Thomas.

Knock it off, girl. You just hooked up with Nik last week before he dumped you for good. You don't need the drama of falling for Nik's younger brother. It's too soon. You don't need to drag Alek into your family's problems.

"There's nothing to slow down for, Alek. My sister's in trouble, again, and she expects me to fill whatever hole she's dug for herself."

She slid the console off her lap again and stood, forcing Alek to let go of her hands. The sudden coolness of the air replacing his warmth bothered her, but she forced herself to ignore the sharp sense of loss.

Alek stood with her. "Why didn't I know that you have a sister? There's nothing in your records about a sister."

He sounded incredulous, as if she had deliberately kept a secret from him. "Half-sister. I have six of them, last I counted. None of them have alternative abilities, and I have no legal ties to them. I haven't even met any of them, except for Octavia. There's no reason for any of them to be in my record."

"Six?" Alek's incredulous tone turned to hurt.

"We all share the same father, but different mothers." She could only guess what Alek would think about that.

"Like my family." Alek nodded toward a family picture sitting on the half wall leading to the kitchen. Far enough away that no one would notice unless he pointed it out. "I mean, Cory has a different father than me, Evan, and Nik."

"I guess." The location of Alek's family portrait invited questions, but she would ask him later. Scott's connection to the Blackwoods had never really been a secret, but when he moved to Star Haven, everyone had forgotten about him. At least they'd forgotten until he crossed Mystic Bay with Hannah, causing havoc for Thunder City. "Except Scott's father died. My father..."

"Your father, what?" Alek prompted.

Serena sighed. "I'm the oldest. My Alt abilities manifested when I was four and my father went berserk."

"Turned anti-Alt, you mean?" Alek guessed.

It should only have been that simple. She could handle anti-Alts. At least, she thought she could with T-CASS at her back. "No, the opposite. He thought I was the greatest daughter in the all the world. We had such fun playing together. By the time I was five, I could create frisbees with light and toss them across the yard. Over time, I could create light spheres of all sizes, and even a rudimentary light slide. Dad was always there to make sure I didn't fall off my slides, or hit the dog while tossing a ball of light, that sort of thing."

Alek motioned for her to sit back down. She might as well, she thought. Alek deserved answers, and she would have to respond to Tavia at some point, which meant staying in the game. "He sounds great, but I also know your parents are divorced."

"True." Serena fiddled with the console paddles laying nearby. "My dad thought I was great, but he wanted more kids. Specifically, he wanted more Alt kids. Mom...didn't. She thought handling me and my ability was hard enough. So, Dad left, met another woman and got her pregnant. This woman already had an Alt child, so I guess he was hedging his bets. When their child didn't manifest powers by the age of four, Dad ditched her a found someone else. They had Octavia, but when she also didn't display any special ability by four, he went on the search for an Alt girlfriend who would give him an Alt child. There are six of us now, and as far as I know, he's still searching. He's determined to have more than one Alt child to boast about."

"Damn." Alek shoved his hands in his pockets. "That's harsh."

Serena shrugged. "He contacts me after every raid. He wants the details of my heroics to brag to his friends. I ignore him, but he begs anyway. Octavia's the only sister with whom I've had any contact, and that was only because her mother couldn't handle her. With Dad on his fourth or fifth girlfriend, Tavia either had to stay with my mom or go into foster care. Neither arrangement lasted long, and she wound up in juvie anyway. When she was released, she stayed with a distant aunt."

The last thing she wanted was pity, but there it was in Alek's eyes.

"I'm sorry. I didn't know any of this. I would have..."

"What?" Her anger mixed with her usual impatience, which she did try to control, but it was hard. "Given me a more responsible father? I have my mother, and that suits me just fine."

Serena stared at the TV screen, where her avatar sat on the ground, waiting for her orders. She wanted to give those orders. She wanted to play the game. Play without guilt hanging around her shoulders because her sister needed her. Or without feeling guilty that she wasn't downtown, organizing the clean-up of the hospital. "I can't stay, Alek. I'm sorry. I need to find Octavia. I need to figure out whatever trouble she's caused and fix it."

She should have stood up again at that point, but she hesitated too long. She didn't want to stand. Her legs wouldn't move, now that she'd unburdened herself onto Alek. Poor Alek sat close enough to place one of those large, warm hands on her shoulder. "Let me help you."

"Why?"

Alek's face tightened, but she wasn't sure of the cause. His hand moved from her shoulder to her arm with a gentle squeeze. "Look at you."

Serena checked her uniform. She hadn't spilled her drink on herself, and there were no stray crumbs. If she'd thought to bring her gym bag she could have changed, but the hadn't. What was Alek seeing that she wasn't?

"No." Alek's voice interrupted her self-exam. "I don't mean what you're wearing, though being seen in uniform probably isn't a good idea right now. I meant you're upset and angry and not thinking straight. That's not like you."

Not thinking straight? No one had ever accused her of that. She'd be insulted, except it was Alek sitting there looking so earnest.

"Your sister contacted you through the game. It can't be that much of an emergency if she's sending messages in-game. Do you have her phone number?"

"Not a current one. I tried calling her on her birthday, but the number had been disconnected."

"Okay, then. Let's get you back into the game. You can reply and ask for more information. For all you know, she just wants assistance with a dungeon run or side quest. Don't overthink this until you have more information."

He had a point. It had been years since she'd spoken to her sister. Maybe Octavia had changed? The attempt at a birthday call had been a whim, mostly because her mother had asked. Despite their failure to help Octavia, her mother did occasionally ask after her.

At any rate, Alek was right. Octavia loved to stir up trouble, so Serena had assumed the worst. "Okay, let's give it try."

Alek handed her the console. Serena angled her avatar back to the mailbox and typed her reply:

Help how?

If her sister could act obtuse, so could Serena. If it was just attention Octavia wanted, then giving it to her at the offset would shorten their contact, and maybe Serena wouldn't have her life interrupted.

"Okay, nothing we can do but wait." Even as she spoke, the mailbox pinged with a message. Tavia must have sent the message before Serena sent her reply.

Boss pwned me. Intends to wipe party. Need to shed aggro too and gain a power spike. Bring guild? Remember Cici.

Serena stared at the words. Most of the message was common gaming language, except for the last sentence, but there was no context for it.

"I don't understand." Alek leaned toward the screen as if that would make the message clearer.

What could Tavia be up to? "You and me both."

"Let's break it down," Alek said. "But start from the end. Who's Cici? I don't recall any boss named Cici. There wouldn't be a boss called Cici. Not in this game."

"It's not a boss. It's a doll." At least she hoped that's what Tavia was referring to. "Tavia had a doll Dad gave her when she was born. The doll's name was Cecilia, but she couldn't pronounce it, so she called it Cici. My mom kept it safe when Tavia went to juvie. When Tavia was released, I was able to sneak the doll to her before Social Services sent her to a temporary foster home until her aunt could pick her up. One of the other kids in the home got hold of Cici and tossed her into a huge commercial garbage bin at the complex where they lived. I got a panicked phone call from Tavia begging me to rescue the doll."

"Did you?"

"Of course." Why would Alek think she wouldn't? "But not before causing a heap of trouble for both of us. I had to leave school for the day to go dumpster diving for the damn doll. Tavia was a teenager at that point. She shouldn't have needed the doll, but she was hysterical."

"But you did get it?"

Serena tried not to roll her eyes. "Have you ever known me to fail?"

"Nope. Not you. Not ever."

"Thanks for the validation." Not that she needed it, but it felt good to hear from someone other than her mother. "It sounds like she wants a rescue, but can't ask outright."

"But why ask you?"

She could see Alek trying to approach the problem from a logical point of view. The problem was that Tavia always acted on her emotions first, not her logic — if she even possessed any. If she wanted to eat a cookie, she ate the cookie, never thinking that maybe the cookie would be nice to have as a dessert after dinner. Then she would throw a tantrum if everyone else ate their cookies after dinner in front of her.

"And why send me the message in-game? She couldn't have known if I was playing."

"Unless you're on her friends list." Alek picked up his

controller. "She would have seen you when you activated your avatar."

"So, the real question is — why would I be on her friends list? We haven't talked in four years. After I rescued the doll, the foster parents called Social Services and they threatened to have me arrested if I didn't stay away from her. They blamed my mom for Tavia's failures because...I don't know, maybe because I was an Alt and took up too much of her time. My mom didn't want to abandon Tavia, but she wouldn't risk losing me.

"Since I had to go dumpster diving to rescue Cici, she probably expects me to pull her out of whatever dumpster fire she started this time, but for some reason can't contact me directly."

Alek didn't respond right away, running his thumb along his lip, deep in thought. "What if someone is monitoring her? Someone she's playing the game with. They could have access to her account. That would be able to read her in-game messages and it would explain why the message is coded in gaming references."

Sickness overtook Serena, because Alek's guess made sense. "That would be completely like her."

"It's okay, Serena." Soft massaging fingers rubbed her shoulder, and for a moment she let Alex's attempt to relax her work on her strained muscles. "We'll figure this out. We'll track her down and find her."

"How? You're not a private investigator like Nik. You're not a cop like Scott. You're not even a hacker like Thomas. What could you possibly do to track her down?"

The genuine hurt on his face made her want to capture all her words and pull them back.

Oh, shit. What have I done?

"You're right." He pulled his hand from her shoulder. "I'm not much of anything. I review computer equipment and software programs, but other than that, I'm just a tool in my mother's toolbox of city defenders."

"I'm sorry, Alek. I didn't mean..."

"No, you're right. It's partly my fault. Half my life I spend flying over the city with Evan, the other half I'm out clubbing with him. We have a reputation. It's a reputation that has its benefits, but it also has drawbacks. No one takes me seriously unless I'm flying around saving people."

"That's not — " But she couldn't finish the sentence before he turned away from her, concentrating on the game again.

"No one in my family can help right now," he said, not looking at her. "The hospital bombing takes precedence for everyone not on leave. We'll only contact Nik if we can't figure this out on our own. I might not be a PI or a crack hacker, but I can find my way through a gaming system well enough. If you trust me?"

"I do," Serena said without hesitation, but she also turned away from Alek so she wouldn't get caught staring. She did believe in him, and would rebuild his faith in her. Later. She would fix this after she found Octavia. "Okay. What should we do first?"

HE SHOULDN'T HAVE SAID any of those things to Serena. He hadn't meant to but having her brush him off in favor of Nik — hell, even Cory — cut deep. He knew he was more than what the public thought of him, but he was still trying to figure out a way to build his own identity without putting Thunder City at risk. The problem was, Thunder City was always at risk. Three anti-Alt attacks in two weeks meant things were going to get a lot worse before they got any better.

No point in dwelling about things he couldn't change, like

what Serena thought of him. He could only change her mind if she wanted her mind to be changed. "This message isn't a request for help in the game. Let's assume that by guild, she means T-CASS. 'Boss pwned me?' Maybe she has a job with a demanding boss?"

"Probably." Serena, at least, had settled back on the sofa. "I can't imagine her working for anyone and not having a persecution complex. 'Intends to wipe party?' I don't think she means a Friday night at a club."

"What if it's not a legal job?" Alek thought back to a few days ago, when Nik had brought Daniella Rose back to the house to meet the family. Dani had a rough-and-tumble past that included more than her fair share of illegal activities. "What if she fell in with the wrong people, and those people intend to hurt others? Maybe she's involved with drugs? Fredek Varga is dead, but I wouldn't be surprised if there were more than one distributor vying to replace him in the blitz trade. Part of Mayor Dane's strategy was to incite a drug war in Star Haven in order to distract from her activities in the quarry."

Serena scrubbed her face with her hands. "God, I hope not. Tavia might have been a pain in the ass when she was a kid, but if her destructive behavior has mutated into criminal activities as an adult...."

"Send her a message back," Alek suggested. "We'll keep in contact with her, play her game until we can find her location. I'll look up her address."

He left Serena alone to craft a game-like message that could tease out what Octavia really wanted or needed. In his bedroom, he pulled out an older laptop, one he had been planning to wipe and dispose of as soon as he found some spare time. He brought it back to the sofa but kept his distance as he booted it up. No point in getting closer to Serena if she still thought Nik was a better choice.

Nik might have had a fancy PI license and access to their father's private investigators firm, but Alek had something better in mind. He performed a quick published records search, but didn't find a listing for her, so he opened his email client and sent several emails until Serena interrupted.

"How does this sound?"

Alek looked up at the screen.

Need Cici coordinates for respawn.

Guild on cool down.

Need stats on AoE.

"Sounds good, but maybe add 'need crafts for critical hit.' It would help if we knew what she was expecting from T-CASS. If she thinks my mom is going to rescue her, she's got another think coming."

Serena added the wording and sent the in-game message. "Who are you emailing?

He'd need to be careful about how he answered that question. "I couldn't find anything in the public records search, so I'm asking a few friends to check the records that aren't online."

"Like what?" Out of the corner of his eye, he could see Serena run her avatar across the screen, collecting a few low level items for crafting. If Octavia was monitoring Serena's avatar, then she would know that Serena was active and waiting for a reply.

"The cable company, the phone company, the courthouse, a couple of newspapers, the banks...just in case someone there has access to an address we could use."

"A skip trace, like what Nik would do? I know he sometimes would bribe people at the phone company for information."

Nik again. "Nothing that formal or intensive, or at least nothing that involves money changing hands."

"If you're going to bribe someone without money, what are you going to offer them? I don't want you to get into trouble."

"I'm not going to get into trouble for taking someone out for a drink."

Serena leaned away from him. "A drink?"

"Yeah, you know, like at a bar."

"You would bribe someone with alcohol?"

He decided not to look at Serena, and kept typing. Let her think what she would about his personal life. She hadn't shown any interest, and now she seemed disgusted. His big chance to get closer to her was shrinking, but if he didn't tell her what he was doing, it would be like lying to her. He didn't want to lie. "Not all of my contacts like hanging out in bars, so maybe dinner and dancing."

"Women? All of your contacts are single women?"

"Yes, all of them are women. I don't know what their current status is." He started a new email. "Why are you so concerned about my contacts? They're just friends."

"Just friends? You'd use your friends like that?"

If he were talking to anyone but Serena, he'd have rolled his eyes by now. "I'm asking them for a favor and offering something in return. We're both getting something out of this."

She didn't say anything, but a quick look at her face, and her perfect posture, made it clear that she thought she knew what he was going to get out of this. Fine. He wasn't shy and he enjoyed having sex. He never promised more than he was willing to give, and most of the women he slept with weren't interested in relationships. They wanted bragging rights. Some didn't even care which twin they banged, so long as they could claim they got to either rumble with Rumble or roar with Roar. Everyone left happy and on good terms, hence the extensive virtual black book he could tap for a favor for a friend. Even a friend he wanted more from.

"Why are you giving me the evil eye?" Though he knew perfectly well why Serena would find his offer to former lady friends in bad taste. "It's not like you didn't know I've had girlfriends."

"I guess I never thought about it much." She shrugged, turning back to the TV, waking up her avatar to keep it active. "I know you have a reputation, but I don't read the gossip rags unless it affects T-CASS business. Even if the rumors were true, I figured you were waiting to find the right person."

If she only knew who the right person was. "I am waiting for the right person, but I'm not going remain celibate while I'm waiting. There's no guarantee the person I love will ever acknowledge me, so why spend my nights lonely, stressed, and miserable?"

He sent the last email, closed the laptop, and met her gaze. What did she want him to say? What *was* he going to say? That he was sorry he'd been enjoying sex since he was sixteen? No. If he ever had a hint that Serena would return any of his affection, he would do everything possible to make her happy, but he wasn't going to apologize for his past. Or even his present.

He wouldn't use his nightmare to guilt trip her into liking him as more than just Nik's brother. She needed to find her own way there, or it wouldn't work. "If it makes you feel better, I haven't hooked up with anyone for a couple of months."

"Months? Really?"

"Yes, months." Why did she look so incredulous? Were his and Evan's reputations that bad? Or, maybe it was only that bad to Serena? "Contrary to what the news rags report, women do turn me down more often than they accept. Despite my notoriety, if I want to spend the night with someone, I still have to work at it. The key is to make them feel valued, so we don't part on bad terms the next morning. Which was why I have an extensive list of contacts to help track down your sister."

Serena looked as if she wanted to say something, but changed her mind, and then changed it back again. "You say you have to work for it, but what about walking away the next day? How do you walk away and not look back? How can you not look back and wonder what you did wrong to not deserve more?"

She had to be talking about Nik, and they must have hooked up before the quarry raid, as he suspected. Well, he deserved that response for being so honest with her about his own hook-ups.

"What makes you think you did something wrong?"

"I'm not talking about. . . ." She stopped because she must have realized denying the obvious was stupid. "Why else would Nik jump out of my bed and into *hers*...if he hadn't thought I'd done something wrong. I mean, we fought about it afterwards. I tried to warn him about Daniella, but he...he really is in love with her. For the first time in my life, I feel like I can't compete with what *she* has to offer him. I've never ever felt as if I had to compete with another woman for a man before. I was always the one who walked away if they didn't meet my expectations. Why now? Why her? Why him?"

Oh, boy. Deep territory. Did he really want to talk about Nik with Serena? Would it help get her get over Nik faster? Would she take him seriously if he confessed to her that he loved her more than Nik ever did? He opened his cider and took a long gulp.

"I don't know Daniella all that well. She was in your class, not mine. I heard a few rumors, but you all were seniors when I was a freshman. I was more interested in the girls I already knew. I only had a few minutes with her when Nik brought her home to meet us."

Serena picked up her cider and took a sip, then another one. "What did you think of her?"

"I thought she had a lot in common with you."

The cider spewed across the coffee table, hitting the gaming controllers. Alek shoved the laptop onto the couch and scooted closer to Serena, patting her on the back until she brought the coughing under control. He stayed close until she took a deep breath, her voice still rough. "How could you possibly think I have anything in common with *her*?"

"It's not an insult."

"She was a *drug dealer*. People died because she sold them *blitz*."

Maybe honesty wasn't such a good idea, but he was already too far along to stop. "She was a minor who was manipulated by an adult. Not to mention, she's found a cure for blitz addiction and is trying to bring it to clinical trials. The statute of limitations on her crimes has passed. If she and Nik get married, I can't have a relationship with my brother and keep on thinking the worst about his wife. I made that mistake with Cory before, and despite the way I treated him, he was the one who stood by me when I needed someone. I won't make that mistake again."

Serena shoved herself off the couch and headed for the kitchen, just as the memory loop started again for Alek. Talking about how Cory had held his hand when he was neck-deep in grief had been a mistake. Cory had been at the harbor. Thinking about him made Alek think about Evan. The image of Evan falling into the inferno flashed in his mind. Save Evan, or save Serena? He ground his palms into his eyes.

Searing heat from the blast. Horror as I watch Evan fall. Pain as my leg brakes.

I need this.

Heat. Horror. Pain.

I need her.

Heat. Horror. Pain.

Repeat. *Heat. Horror. Pain.*

And again. And again. Faster.

How can I justify my decision to save her over Evan if I screw this up? Don't screw this up, damn it.

"Alek, what's wrong?"

The nightmare receded but didn't disappear. He stopped grinding his hands into his eyes, letting them drop. Serena had returned with a fist full of paper towels crunched in her hand. Why was he not surprised that she would think to clean up immediately after making a mess, instead of acknowledging their fight? Hell, it was their first fight and they weren't even dating.

"Sorry. I've been getting headaches since the harbor attack. It's mild. I just need to close my eyes for a minute."

He leaned his head back, but his body was very aware of Serena reaching across him to wipe the cider off the table.

"You should see the medic at HQ about that."

Nope. That was not going to happen. He could handle this — would handle this — in his own way. He didn't need a medic or doctor telling him what he already knew: the only people responsible for what happened at the harbor were the anti-Alt terrorists. Whatever choices he had to make in the heat of the moment were on their shoulders, not his.

If only he could get his emotions to sync up with what his brain.

When he heard Serena toss the paper towels into the garbage bucket near the television, he opened his eyes again. She sat next to him.

"Better?" she asked.

"Yeah, it's like lightning — hits me fast and hard, then disappears. I'm okay now. It's like it never happened."

Liar.

Shut up, I'm fine.

His conscience did as he ordered, for now.

Serena must have believed him because he could still see she was angry with him. "Tell me, in very precise terms, what I have in common with...with...*her*."

Serena was riled up, so getting farther away was his best bet to not get hit with a light sphere, or another memory loop. He slid back, pulling his legs up on the sofa, so he could turn to face her. "You're both passionate about what you care about. I mean, look at you. You were ready to fly out of here to track your sister down, in uniform no less. You would have chewed up seventy-two hours of your free time, trying to find someone who hasn't had the courtesy to contact you in four years. All over what might not have been anything more than a request for help with a boss fight."

"I could have tried harder to stay in touch." Serena picked up her cider for another sip. "I *should* have tried harder."

"She wasn't your responsibility." Alek had memorized Serena's T-CASS history. If anyone could remind her of her successes, he could. "You had your own responsibilities. You joined T-CASS before you graduated high school. You applied for and completed the toughest Special Operations Exam on your first try and in record time. No one who hasn't already had years of experience has ever done that. No one since has been allowed to join before they turned eighteen. You're a legend. Taking care of a half-sister might have been your mother's choice, but it shouldn't have become yours.

"As for Daniella, when she talks about her work, it's as if nothing else in the room exists, not even Nik. Same with you. When you're determined to rescue someone, you assess the situation and take action. I read all of your after-action reports. Every decision you've ever made has been rooted in logic and a profound sense of responsibility to keep people safe."

Serena ran her thumb around the lip of the cider bottle, pouting. "She has a Ph.D. All I have is a Bachelor's in Management."

Damn, her confidence must have taken quite a beating in the wake of Daniella Rose. Daniella was a force of nature, but Serena was just as fierce, if not more so because of her commitment to T-CASS. She spent her days taking care of others: the Newcomers, her teammates, her friends. Who was there in her life to take care of her?

"There's a bullshit excuse, if I ever heard one." Alek gulped down the rest of his cider. "All my mom has is a high school diploma. You want to call Captain Spec stupid? Good luck with that."

She kept her focus on her bottle, but he could tell she was thinking over his words.

"Another thing you have in common is you're both sexy as hell." It must have been the cider talking, because he sure hadn't planned on telling her that.

"What?" Oh, now she had her *"don't you give me a crap answer"* look on her face.

"I said, you're both – "

"I heard you the first time, but hell, Alek, you're a..."

"Don't you dare say *kid*." He pointed the bottle tip at her. "I haven't been a kid for at least a decade."

"I know that, but you've always been Nik's younger brother to me and. . . ." She stopped talking.

Fuck it all to hell. I should have been the one to drop into the fire. Alek kept that thought to himself.

She actually looked guilty now. "Wow...I'm sorry."

Which didn't make Alek feel any better, because the point of this discussion was to bolster Serena's confidence, not his. She was so close that Alek couldn't stand it. The temptation of having her lips just inches away. . . he couldn't help himself, so he leaned over and kissed her.

3

THE SOFT BRUSH of his lips against hers hovered after the initial touch, hesitant, waiting for her to decide if she wanted this. If she waited too long, would the unexpected spark disappear? Would she miss the first connection in a long time that brought joy to her heart without her needing a reason, or a plan, or advanced notice? She desperately didn't want to lose this feeling, so with a slight tilt to her head, her lips brushed his, surrendering to the unexplained desire surging through her.

Alek slid closer with her consent so that he could reach for her, his hands cupping her cheeks, taking advantage of the limited space on the sofa and drawing her into a more intimate kiss. The taste of cider blossomed on her tongue, the sharpness tugging away her guilt, making her forget her past failures, and giving her a sense of emotional pleasure she hadn't experienced in so long.

This had to be foolish. She was still heartbroken over Nik. Wasn't she?

Well, maybe not, because she didn't try to stop Alek from sliding his lips down to her neck, his tongue tickling her pulse point. All she did was let loose a long moan and drag him closer, and the other hand clawing at his shoulder. Why didn't she push him away? Why was she leaning back and pulling him on top of her? Why did he slip his around her to push the throw pillow behind her onto the floor?

She wanted this, as a reminder that she didn't need to hang her gloves on the dick of a man who would never appreciate her, no matter how hard she tried. Alek appreciated her. He always had; every time she joined him, either in a game, or an operation, or at his parent's house for a party. They had worked together enough times that each one knew how the other one thought, which made the T-CASS raids so much easier when she didn't have to explain everything in fine detail. Alek would know what to do and his twin would join him.

He sure knew what do to now. Only someone with experience in removing a T-CASS uniform would know where to find the clasp to release the form-fitting material. With a snap and a tug, he had the top of her uniform peeled back, exposing her down to her waist.

Well, turnabout was fair play, so she yanked up his t-shirt until he was forced to release her and pull it over his head. The cool air of the apartment made the loss of his warm hands on her all the more noticeable. She took a moment to admire the fine man Alek had become. Of course, it wasn't the first time she'd seen Alek shirtless, but this time she took notice of the details: the extra-wide shoulders; the fine dusting of hair that started at his chest and worked its way down to his jeans; the muscles that were ripped from his pecs to his abs, which she had known were there, but had never appreciated before now.

Her rumination stopped when Alek slipped her bra straps off her shoulders and unhooked the clasp. His hands, oh, God those hands, strong and firm as they massaging her breasts. The sofa was wide enough to keep her comfortable, but for what her body craved, was it big enough?

Any thoughts she had about not following through with what she'd started ended when Alek slipped his hands under the lower half of her uniform.

"Bed." She managed to speak the command despite the fireworks in her brain. "Now."

He slid off of her, but instead of helping her to her feet, he created a pillow of air to lift her body from the sofa and into his arms. He carried her into the bedroom, which was larger than her entire apartment. Even with the lights dimmed she could see the problem: boxes were everywhere, even on the king-sized bed. That didn't stop Alek. He balanced her in the air once more. Another wave of his hand, and a sharp wind tumbled the boxes off the bed and onto the floor.

That kind of control over his ability only made her hotter. Any thoughts other than getting Alek inside her disappeared. He lowered her to the bed and resumed where they had left off, except now she had room to stretch. Touching him, stroking him, kissing him, renewed her sense of self. Her strength. Her determination. She hadn't become the youngest member of T-CASS by wallowing in a corner and giving into her doubts and fears. She had succeeded by confronting her doubts, cornering her fears, and stomping them into the ground until the leeching of her best self had stopped.

Her hands wandered down to his backside, perfect for grabbing, with a quick shove to keep the front of him in place while she gave him more room to maneuver between her legs.

"One sec," he whispered in her ear before rolling off her and reaching for a nightstand.

One second for what? Damn it, she wanted his ass back in her grasp — but then she heard the wrapper and realized what he was doing. A part of her relaxed even further knowing Alek was protecting her, though she used her own form of protection as well.

He returned exactly where he had left off, sliding a single finger down her abdomen to create friction right where she needed it the most. Right...there. He rubbed in an arrhythmic teasing fashion, bringing her close until she thrust against him, then slowing down and frustrating her, then speeding back up. She tried to grab his backside again, to force him even closer until he finished, but he used his leverage to pin her back on the bed.

She gave in and let him have his way with her body. He took full advantage by licking each of her nipples, withholding satisfaction from her until she squeezed her knees against him, begging him to enter her.

"Not yet," he whispered. "Keep it slow."

Another moan escaped her lips as he removed his finger from inside of her.

"Alek, please..." Was she actually begging him? She'd never begged, not for any of her lovers, not for...anyone. If he wanted to play games, she could give as much as she got.

With a push, she maneuvered her hand between their bodies, sealed so close together than she couldn't miss her target once she slid lower along the hard planes of his torso. She pinched the tip of him with a light touch before wrapping her hand around the rest.

The sharp intake of breath told her she had achieved her revenge. Now it was her turn to set the pace, stroking him slow enough to make him squirm before speeding up, bringing him to the edge, then slowing back down again.

"You're...a...demoness..."

She placed her other hand back where it belonged — on the solid muscles of his backside. He whispered her name over and over again. She could feel the growl build from low in his chest, where she had laid her head.

One final stroke turned his growl into a moan. Before he

finished, she wrapped her legs around him slipping back underneath his body with an inviting sigh of her own.

The loss of his own pleasure brought him back to hers. His finger returned to her, the rhythm matching her heartbeat, the desire inside her rising, turning into something else, something she couldn't define because she'd never felt it before. It was more than pleasure, more than happiness, more than a loss of control.

With a one last teasing pinch denying her the friction she desperately needed, he slipped inside of her, filling her, but not quite satisfying her. Not yet, not until he—

Her hands began to glow...her control...she was losing control! But she couldn't stop him from rocking back and forth, building the pressure, the pleasure spreading within and without.

She tried to warn Alek, but she couldn't find the words. Her gasps stole her voice; her craving for her climax buried her logic with desperate need. The satisfaction of the friction scraping across her skin overrode her attempts to stop herself from letting go of everything.

She fell over the edge with a blast of light that shattered his mirror and overhead fan.

Alek finished with a sweet cry of his own, but she wasn't sure if it was from her the light or his orgasm. His eyes were shut tight as he eased to a slower pace before lowering himself onto her.

They lay together, his breath tickling her ear.

"I've never...that has never happened before." She still couldn't believe it.

Alek pulled out of her, and rolled to the side, his hand now stroking her hair. She must have lost her yellow-feathered barrette somewhere along the way.

"That was incredible." He kissed her cheek, his fingers

wandering from her hair down to her forehead, over her nose and chin. "You are incredible. I still can't believe you allowed me to make love with you."

Serena swallowed. He sounded as if he'd wanted this to happen before today. "How long?"

"Eleven and a half inches, according to the *Thunder City Sizzler*."

"What?" Then she realized what he was talking about, so she whacked his chest with the back of her knuckles. "No, I mean, how long have you...I mean, you didn't just decide to sleep with me in the past fifteen minutes, did you?" She held her breath, not knowing if she really wanted this to be just a spur of the moment hook-up or something more. She didn't want to hope or guess either way because she wasn't sure herself.

"Oh, well...." he pulled part of the sheet from the other side of the bed, and covered his so-called eleven and a half inches. "I decided I wanted to sleep with you on my thirteenth birthday, when you played the original *Battleguards* with me instead of eating birthday cake."

"That long?" He had better not be joking this time, but this was Alek. A cute quip was about the extent of his humor. His hand returned to trace a path down her body, oh so slow and deliberate.

"When I first met you," he said, "it was only a crush. Once we got to playing the game, though, and I realized you really knew what you were doing, and you didn't mind that I was three years younger than you...I knew you were worth waiting for. Even I could tell the difference back then."

He looked at her as if she really was worth waiting for.

"I don't know what to say," she said.

"Well, I'm known for leaving women speechless, or so the *Sizzler* reports."

"Do you always read the *Sizzler*?" She raised her head off the pillow, just enough to twist around and look at him.

He knitted his brows together. "Daily. How else could I keep track of my love life if they didn't document everything?"

"I can't imagine what they're going to say when they find out about this." She laid her head back so she could see the burnt ceiling fan. "And we can't let anyone know about *that*. I could lose my position at T-CASS, and then what would I do?"

Alek scooted closer, slipping an arm around her until they were spooned together. "Don't worry. I'll tell management that I tried to change one of the lightbulbs and electrocuted myself."

"Think they'll buy a story like that?"

He shrugged. "The management company for this place gets enough in rent to understand the meaning of the word '*discretion*.' It's not like I trash the place on a regular basis, puke in the hallways every weekend, or blast hard rock at high volume all night."

Serena nodded. "I guess we should clean up and check to see if Octavia responded."

Alek snuggled closer to her. "I don't want to let you go."

She didn't want to hurt him or break the mood for herself, but she didn't know what *this* meant for her. After so many years of dating Nik, and dating others in between dating Nik, how could she know for sure that this was anything other than physical relief from working so hard? Could she even trust her instincts at this point?

Instead of talking about her insecurities, she kissed his nose. "Sorry pal, but if I'm going to get that uniform on again, I'm going to need a shower at least."

He grunted but released her. "Um, this is awkward, but there's some clothes in the bedroom across the hallway that might fit."

"Do I want to know why you have women's clothes in your closets?"

He shrugged. "Sometimes they get left behind by accident. Or sometimes, they get left behind deliberately on the assumption that their owners would be coming back."

Typical. "I'm not sure I want to wear your ex-girlfriends' clothing."

"Up to you." He stood up...oh, well, he might actually be eleven and a half inches. "But I figure if you can find a few casual pieces, those would be more comfortable than the uniform and won't draw attention if we head out to find your sister. Everything is clean, in case you change your mind."

"All right. I'll give them a try." She pulled away, scooped up her uniform, and headed for the other bedroom. It lacked any furniture except for a bed, a desktop computer, a closet, and was the size of a cavern. The full bathroom was larger than her own bedroom. It was also stocked with the essentials, including a shower cap, so she didn't have to worry about her hair. The high-powered jets massaged her tired muscles, while dispelling the evidence of sex and sweat. After she'd dried off, she checked the closet.

It was filled from top to bottom. She wasn't a prude, but good heavens, how many girls had Alek brought back here? Nothing to do about it. She tried a few pairs of jeans first, but they were all too big. Alek must like women on the bigger side, because though she was physically fit, she wasn't a tiny woman, especially around the hips, not like...

Nope. She was not going down the road of comparing herself to Daniella. Daniella was a shifter, so who knew what her real size was, anyway?

The third pair of jeans fit snugly enough to stay on her hips without the need for a belt. Finding a shirt was easier as Alek also seemed to prefer bustier women. Good to know, as she pulled on a pink short-sleeved t-shirt just long enough to still be considered fashionable.

There were even shoes lining the bottom of the closet. Luck of the draw, she found a pair of sneakers in her size, with socks already stored in the box. She hoped the owner didn't come back looking for them.

She hoped the owner didn't come back, period.

Well, that's a pretty possessive thought for someone who's still hung up on Nik.

Serena yanked the shoelaces into a tight knot.

Nik never made me lose control over my ability like Alek did.

Oooooo, someone's in love again...

Shut up.

She ignored the make-up sitting in a cardboard box and marched out to the living room. Alek sat on the sofa, laptop in place.

"Mom called," he said with his eyes on the computer. "Thomas is sleeping off the anesthesia, so she's staying at the hospital. Cory's called Garrett to pick him up at the Arena. Hannah's still missing, and Nik is fine, in case you were wondering."

His tone was too careful, too neutral, for her not to know that he didn't want to talk about Nik at all.

"I never doubted his ability to slip away from trouble, even if it was a bomb."

She slid onto the sofa, closer to Alek than was necessary, and kissed his cheek. He looked at her and smiled, wide and honest. She found herself smiling back. The ping on his computer put a stop to any thoughts of continuing their conversation—or anything else for that matter.

Serena checked her in-game inbox, so she wouldn't think too much about who was emailing Alek. No response to her last message yet.

"We have a lead," Alek said as he typed on the computer.

Serena blanked the TV screen so she could focus on Alek. "From who?"

Alek leaned in for a quick kiss. "No names, because that's not important. Let's just say a friend of mine at the cable company says she spotted someone at Cybervid Games, near Bolton Park, who looked a lot like you."

"Cybervid Games. I've heard of them." Serena closed her eyes to remember where from. "I saw a few ads on TV. They're independent, not a chain. And they're too far away from both HQ and my apartment for my convenience."

"Yeah, my friend said she was there to fix the Wi-Fi system. Here's what she says about it: *I got the creepiest feeling while I was there. The owner has a room in back, almost like a call center, with rows and rows of different gaming systems, far more than any other gaming stores I've visited. There were, well, not kids—older teens and young adults back there, waiting for me to fix the system. I think they worked there, but I can't imagine why. The big gaming companies have clamped down on token farming and power leveling over the years, so it's really not profitable anymore. Anyway, if this Octavia you're looking for is the girl I saw, she's part of whatever it was they were doing.*"

Serena pondered the words. "I never thought Tavia resembled me at all, but I guess sharing a father...."

Alek closed the laptop and pulled one of her hands into his. "We should go check out Cybervid Games."

"Not in uniform." No more playing around with her career. "Nothing official. T-CASS doesn't investigate crimes." Not that Alek needed reminding.

"Not to mention we're both recognizable." He rubbed his thumb along her knuckles.

Oh, boy, did she need to find her focus, because Alek could talk her into anything if he kept it up with the touching.

"How about we just wander down there," he continued as if turning her on was no big thing, "and see if there's a way we can watch who goes in and who goes out. If we see your sister — we'll find a way to talk to her on the street."

Serena nodded. "Sounds like a plan. Do you own any hats?"

"Hats?"

She thought he looked cute when he was confused. "Like a disguise. As you said, we're recognizable."

"Sure, as long as you root for the Tornadoes." He pulled his hand from hers as he reached into an end table drawer and pulled out a baseball cap.

"As if I'd root for anyone else."

~

OCTAVIA ALMOST DIDN'T MAKE it into the bathroom. It took a while, but she finally managed to send another message to Serena pretending she was messaging new recruit. After she sent the note, she signaled to Mister Kolar that she needed a bathroom break. Breaks were regulated so that there were a minimum of five employees in the game at any time, just in case a recruit got cold feet. There always had to be someone available to talk them out of leaving too soon, or before committing to one of their parties.

Once in the bathroom, she locked the door. It was a single toilet stall, so she was alone for now. This was probably the only place in the whole building where she wouldn't be monitored or watched.

She pulled her hands from her pockets. The smoke still billowed from her fingertips, but not so much that she couldn't hide it. Typing on the keyboard thinned out the smoke. Plus, with everyone else hunched over their own gaming systems, no one noticed. She still had to find a way to make it stop, but how? What should she do?

This hadn't happened since her seventh birthday. The one her father couldn't attend because his other daughter — Serena — had just started dating one of the Blackwood sons and he was too busy trying to get an invite to the Blackwood estate. He hadn't seen the wisps circling her fingers then, and her mother had been too high on blitz to notice.

Octavia had waved her fingers in the air, her thoughts turning darkening at her inability to make this strange magic stop. Serena was the only sister her father ever wanted to talk about — Serena this and Serena that. He wouldn't shut up about her. Serena had Alt powers, she could summon light, and she could save the world. She would marry the son of one of the most powerful Alts in the world, and a trust fund baby to boot.

Back then, Octavia hadn't known what to do, so she had shoved her hands into a pot soaking in the sink. She pulled her hands out every couple of minutes until the smoke stopped on its own. As she had told the kid in the game, the only Alt powers that counted in Thunder City were the useful powers that could save people. Even at the age of seven, she knew generating little puffs here and there would never save her, or anyone else, so she never told anyone about what had happened. Eventually, the memory faded under the weight of foster care and living with her better-than-sliced-bread sister. The smoke never appeared again.

Until today.

Her doubts about Mister Kolar's set-up had started to sprout two weeks ago, when T-CASS attacked the hidden quarry prison in Star Haven. He'd called them all together so they could mourn the fallen normal soldiers who had valiantly defended themselves against the attacking alternative humans. Octavia mourned and contributed to the collection jar, but the more reports she heard over the news feed, the more it sounded as if Star Haven's mayor had been working with Alts to create even more Alts by changing their genetics.

That flew in the face of everything Mister Kolar had taught her. Anyone who associated with an alternative human had to be a sympathizer and was not to be trusted. Mayor Dane had done more than just associate; she worked with Alts and even had an Alt daughter.

She had wanted to ask Mister Kolar questions about that, but with preparations for the party Friday night in full swing, there wasn't much of a chance to ask him in private. Asking him in front of the other employees was out of the question. Every teacher she'd ever known had made it clear that she wasn't smart enough to ask questions about anything without annoying the whole class. It was easier to keep her mouth shut, or run away, or drop out.

Now she was stuck in the bathroom running cold water over her hands, praying that the smoke would stop.

Knock, knock, knock.

"Tavia, are you okay in there?"

It was Mister Kolar. Smoke still billowed from her fingers, but not quite as obviously as before. She opened the door a crack, so Mister Kolar could only see her head.

"I'm okay, Mister K. It's just...well...it's that time of month and um, I've got some serious cramps. Could I just have a few more minutes until the painkillers start to work?"

He gave her that half-smile. "Okay, Tavia. Do what you need to do. Those painkillers won't interfere with your Bupropion, will it?"

The look of honest concern on his face tried to wrap a sense of security around her, but more doubts beat it back. Mister Kolar knew she had a problem with depression. She'd been honest with him when he'd first hired her, because she'd gotten fired from a couple of jobs before. He'd told her that her schedule would be flexible enough that she could still see her therapist when she needed to, and she would have enough leave time if she really couldn't report to work.

She had never told him which anti-depressant she was taking.

"No, Mister K. I'll be fine. I already asked the doc about it."

He nodded and walked away, allowing her to close the door. She looked down at her hands. The smoke was gone. Maybe the distraction was enough to stop it? She didn't know.

From her back pocket, she pulled out her cell phone — another item she couldn't have afforded without this job. She checked the mobile app that allowed her to access her game account. Serena hadn't responded yet to her second message, and Octavia didn't have her sister's number. She'd lost it a long time ago and figured she'd never need it again.

Serena had saved her doll back then. She'd had also raced under the floating container to save the crew of the cargo ship. A part of Octavia still hated Serena for being perfect, but Octavia also knew she was over her head in trouble again and she needed her big sister to rescue her.

Her teachers were right — she really was a stupid girl.

"Now, what?" Serena looked around, adjusting her plastic visor with the Tornado team logo, while she tried to pull her other hand out of his. "I don't know this neighborhood at all."

They leaned against the bricks just on the edge of a door leading into a convenience store across the street from Cybervid Games. They stood close, acting like they were having a moment. Alek tugged her hand back. "Keep your hand in mine."

"I'm not sure that's a good idea." She didn't pull her hand away, though.

"I am." After thirteen years of waiting for Serena, he wasn't about to let go of her hand so fast. He only wished he could shout to the world how much she meant to him.

"You know better than me what your sister looks like. Can you see over my shoulder?"

Serena stepped a couple of inches to her left. "Now I can. You're too damn big, Blackwood."

"Family trait."

"No kidding."

He laughed, having missed her sarcasm. He wanted more of it. He wanted more of *her*, but he also knew Serena could not be contained. Her dedication to T-CASS was rivaled only by his mother's. For a second, he imagined Serena picking up the reins of T-CASS, should his mother ever give them up. If she did, he'd stand by her side, regardless of his own ambitions — which he'd have to reconsider anyway, if they were going to be a couple.

Five minutes passed. A group of young people headed into Cybervid Games, but no one came out. Ten minutes. Serena shifted from one foot to the other. The after-work crowd started streaming into the convenience store for pre-packaged dinners. Had terrorist attacks become so common that folks just carried on as if it meant nothing?

"We can't stand out here forever," Serena muttered.

"Check the game app. See if we can send a message that would let her know we're out here."

Serena pulled out her phone, activated the app, and started typing. "Still no message from her." She typed again. "Sent her another note, but it might be too vague."

They waited another fifteen minutes. A garbage truck rumbled past, braked and turned into a short side street to pick up a commercial dumpster. Alek ignored the grinding of the hydraulics until the top of the dumpster slammed closed.

Explosion. Serena below him, Evan falling. Who to save? Who to save? Make your choice.

"Alek? *Alek?*"

Serena's voice. She was shaking him because he had mashed his hands into his eyes to drive out the scene. To stop himself from having to make the choice again.

"Sorry." Serena grabbed his hands and pulled them both against her chest, her fingers massaging his knuckles. The garbage truck lifted a second dumpster, and that top dropped too.

Serena. Evan. Heat. Pain. Choose.

"I'm sorry." He pulled his hands away from her to cover his eyes again. He wasn't sure who he was apologizing to — the Serena in front of him, the Serena in his mind's eye, or Evan as he fell into the flames.

Pain. No. Wait. Pain. Serena in the here and now was digging her nails into his biceps.

"Snap out of it, Blackwood."

His eyes shot open. Serena stood there with a mixture of concern, fear, and maybe a little annoyance. "I'm..."

"Yes, I know, you're sorry. You said that, twice."

Alek adjusted his baseball cap. "Did I draw too much attention?"

Serena glanced around. "No, we're fine, but c'mon, Alek. You have a serious problem. You need to see a doctor about those headaches."

"I will." He hunched down more, curling his shoulders to get closer to Serena's lips. "I promise, as soon as we find your sister, I'll..."

Another top dropped.

Choose!

Damn it. The memory flash almost blinded him to everything but Serena's eyes. Her brown eyes, so filled with concern for him. This was what he had made the choice for, so why was his brain fucking it up? "I promise, I'll see a doctor. First thing."

She stood on tiptoe and kissed him. "You better."

The garbage truck accelerated, driving farther down the street, the noise no longer bothersome. Alek relaxed, his arms less tense, his hands finding Serena's once again.

More shoppers entered the convenience store. Someone was bound to recognize them, hats or no hats.

"Let's cross the street." His pain lessened with purpose. He took Serena's arm and approached the crosswalk. The crosswalk signal turned white, so they rushed across as fast as they could without activating their abilities.

"I think that's her." Serena crossed in front of Alek, almost stepping on his toes, to get to the sidewalk perpendicular to Cybervid Games. Alek followed, but he'd lost his place by her side. Serena kept walking toward the small group that had exited the game store. Alek hung back just far enough to give Serena space, but close enough to intervene if the situation fell sideways. Most of the group headed toward them, so they could catch the bus at the stop up the road.

Serena angled herself so her shoulder bumped one of the women, also black, but shorter than Serena. Serena paused only long enough to look at the woman, mutter "sorry," then kept moving.

Alek caught up with her. "Was it her?"

"Yes, and she knows it's me now. Just keep walking to the next corner, then get us up to the roof."

The main street had become crowded, so he waited until they rounded the corner. This particular side road was one way only, and meant for service vehicles making deliveries.

Pedestrians rarely used it, and right now it was empty. Alek waited until they had walked halfway to the next intersection, then full-tilt launched both of them up to the roof.

"This way." Serena tugged at his sleeve. "Back so we're over the front entrance of Cybervid."

Alek let her pull him along until they were on top of the entrance. They both peeked over the edge.

Serena nudged him. "She's coming back."

"How are we going to get her up here without everyone seeing?"

"The same way we did. I'll send her another message through the app."

Alek watched her type the message on the screen. A moment later, Octavia checked her own phone. Her hair, a natural cut with all the curls blowing in the breeze, obscured Alek's ability to see if she was typing a reply or not.

"C'mon, c'mon," Serena whispered. A second later Octavia walked away from the front of the store toward the corner. Alek took the lead this time, with Serena following him to the edge. "Here's hoping she doesn't yell," he said.

He generated a powerful vortex below and pulled as fast as he could. Octavia let out a yip, but he hoped she was on the roof before anyone noticed her disappearance.

"Wha...wha...Serena. You're here." Octavia stumbled as she stepped outside of the dissipating vortex. Alek reached out to pull her away from the edge.

Octavia looked up at him, squinted, and got that look on her face that he saw when folks couldn't tell which twin he was. At this point, no one from street level could see them, so he removed the cap. "Alek Blackwood. Roar."

"Oh." Octavia nodded, but looked past him to her sister. "Thanks, but I thought Serena would bring everyone."

"T-CASS is a little busy, but Alek was available. I asked for his help." Serena reached out to take her sister into a hug. "Are you hurt? Do you need anything?"

Octavia shook her head, hugging Serena back, but not with the wholehearted abundance Alek would expect from sisters who hadn't seen each other in a while. "No, I'm not hurt. I'm not in that kind of trouble."

Serena pulled away, but still giving Octavia a critical look. "We can't stay up here all day long. Can you tell us what's going on?"

"Why don't we get off the roof altogether?" Alek suggested.

"We've already risked being seen twice," Serena pointed out. "We should stay put for the moment."

"Fine, we'll stay on the roof, but how about we all sit, get as comfortable as we can." He took the initiative and sat down where he was. The roof tiles weren't comfortable, but at least it got them all at eye level. He sat closer to Octavia, who looked as if she were about to cry.

"I...I don't know where to start?"

Alek rubbed her arm as a gesture of solidarity, but also to get closer so he could give her a brief exam. He didn't spy any obvious signs of blitz use: her teeth showed no signs of decay, her eyes looked clear, her skin didn't have bloody scabs. Of course, that didn't mean anything if she had just graduated from a milder drug to blitz. Still, he'd take it as a good sign for now.

"I'm an Alt," Octavia declared.

Alek jerked his hand off her. He'd been touching her bare arm. He was damn lucky nothing had happened. If Octavia's ability proved dangerous, he'd have to grab Serena and get her off the roof fast. He thought Serena had said none of her sisters were Alts.

"An Alt?" Serena's face melted from guarded concern to outright sympathy. "Tavia, when did you find this out? How long have you known?"

Tavia leaned back with a sigh of high drama. "I sort of found out when I was seven, but it only lasted for a few minutes. Nothing happened again until today. I swear."

"Seven?" Serena scooted closer to her sister but, like Alek, didn't reach out to touch her sister. "Why didn't you tell me? I could have helped you. I could have trained you."

Tears spilled out of Octavia's eyes. "I know. I should have said something, but I didn't want the attention. I just wanted to disappear. You know what my mom was like. Attention meant I was in trouble again. I was always in trouble. Everything was always my fault."

Alek listened, but said nothing. He wanted to sympathize with Octavia, but he also couldn't help but wonder if this was how Cory felt all those years, after the time-out room incident. Had he thought his brothers locking him in and turning it on was his fault? Was that why he clung so close to Thomas? Was that why he'd left Thunder City altogether?

"Not everything was your fault," Alek found himself saying. Deep down, he knew he had to say the same thing to Cory someday. "You were just mixed up because of your mom. Serena's told me a little bit about your past. Serena's mom tried to help, but you needed more help than she could give."

"I know." Octavia sobbed into her hands. "I didn't know what I wanted — more attention, less attention. I was confused and then the smoke happened, and I panicked. I decided less attention was better."

Serena was quiet while her sister cried, but she wrung her hands, as if eager to put them around her sister. After a while, the tears slowed.

"We'll have to get you registered as soon as possible." Serena started to stand. "You can't live here until you prove you can control your ability."

"How could I not know that, after living with you for two years?"

Whoa, whiplash. Tears to anger in less than a finger snap. Alek moved his feet underneath him, ready to spring if Octavia activated her ability.

Instead, she started yelling. "Little Miss Law and Order, always spewing about the rules. Always rules with you, the good girl who obeyed every rule. Couldn't get away from you fast enough!"

This was getting dangerous. They didn't know how deep Octavia's troubles ran, but if she had become involved with someone who was manipulating her, then drawing their attention would make extricating her more dangerous.

"What's your ability?" Serena's voice held a cautious note, as if she wanted to dig harder for answers, but didn't want to hurt her sister either.

"Smoke comes out of my fingertips. It's a useless ability. I can't save anyone with a cloud of smoke." She held up her hands. "Look, it's starting again. Smoke. Useless smoke."

Sure enough, even in the light of day, Alek could see the wisps of smoke curling into the breeze.

"You don't know that." Alek needed to boost her confidence, keep her calm so if her ability did turn out to be dangerous, she wouldn't hurt them by accident. "Any ability can be useful in the right set of circumstances. You don't need to worry about saving other people right now. We just want *you* to be safe."

Octavia looked at him as if no one had ever offered to keep her safe before. Maybe no one had.

"That's not the problem. The problem is Mister Kolar. He recruited me when I aged out of the system. I needed a job, one that allowed me the flexibility to see my therapist, and a boss who wouldn't fire me every time my depression got the better of me. I'd already gotten fired from three jobs while I was in the system, but I've been working for Mister Kolar for two years. I make a living wage. I have my own apartment. I haven't felt this good since...I can't even tell you when."

"He sounds like an amazing boss." Alek glanced at Serena, who sat there, looking uncertain. She said nothing, so he kept talking. "Why is he a problem?"

Octavia picked at the knot in her shoelace. "He's anti-Alt. Like, extreme anti-Alt. Once I got promoted to the back room where he runs his operation, I discovered that most of his profits go toward supporting the anti-Alt organizations back in Star Haven. Since the Alt ban passed and all the Alts came here, he's been saying that Star Haven has been cleansed, and it's time to focus on getting the Alts out of Thunder City. He calls us soldiers and says we're fighting a war."

"Son of a bitch." Serena scrubbed her face with her hands. "You knew this about him for how long? Why didn't you contact me sooner? You know I would have dropped everything to help you. Just like I did with Cici."

"It's not illegal to be anti-Alt." Octavia pouted and continued to pick at her shoe. "I didn't even think of myself as an Alt. Except for that one time, I haven't generated any smoke, and let me tell you — I wanted to. You think I would have let the cops drag me off to juvie if I could have done something about it?"

"And gotten yourself into bigger trouble." Serena looked ready to kill. "You knew *I* was an Alt. You worked for...no, you supported a man who supports terrorists? You took money from a guy who funds the people who blew up the cargo ship in the harbor, who shot people trying to run away? Who just tried to blow up a hospital filled with patients? Why, Tavia? What did we ever do to you?"

"You think you're so superior to the rest of us. Maybe not all Alts act like you," she had the grace to look at Alek briefly, "but you were obnoxious every time I walked in the room. Your mom treated you like a damned princess, and I was just the poor relation you had to tolerate."

"That's no excuse — "

"All right. Let's stop the bickering." Alek cut Serena off because he couldn't let them go on like this while they were vulnerable. "Kolar's a problem if he's supporting the terrorists who attacked the harbor and the hospital."

"He didn't support those attacks." Octavia picked at her shoelaces, the smoke from her fingertips still spilling out in light wisps. "He's against the blatant violence. He's says it's counter-productive because it forces the city government to support you all."

Alek moved back toward Octavia. "But he's still giving money to those same organizations."

"Or he could be lying to you," Serena pointed out, but at least she leaned back on her hands, a less threatening posture.

"He says that it's better to change hearts and minds." Octavia became more animated, her hands no longer picking at her shoelaces, but waving around with excitement. "He throws parties once a month, usually on Fridays. We recruit during the week. That's literally all we do. We go into a game — for me it's *Battleguards* — and we find other players who might want to hang out with us, and we talk to them about joining our group. As we talk to them, we make it known that we don't like Alts. When they join the party, they see we're really one big family, and they usually join us. If they're loyal, Mister Kolar trains them to work in the back room."

"A recruiter." Serena almost spit as she said the word.

Alek had heard about anti-Alt recruiters from other operations both within Thunder City and elsewhere.

"Great, that's just great." Serena readjusted her legs. "He's brainwashing people using cookies and milk. How much money did you give him, Tavia?"

"Hey, he paid me when no one else would." Octavia started to stand, but Alek managed to get ahold of her shirt sleeve and kept her down. He wasn't sure if she even noticed. "I needed a job that would allow me to manage my mental health. Mister Kolar treated me right when no one else would."

"So what are we doing here?" Alek let go of her shirt. "Why did you reach out to us? Why are you asking for help?"

Octavia held up her hands, nearly shoving them into Alek's face. The smoke still billowed from her fingers, curling around her knuckles until the light breeze caught the tendrils and pulled them higher, until they disappeared. "I can't control it. I couldn't let Mister Kolar see this; I can't keep my hands in my pockets all day long, either. I had to hide in the bathroom until it stopped, but now it's starting again."

She sounded so miserable; he couldn't help his own empathy toward the girl.

"Let's get you back to your apartment, Octavia." Alek nodded at Serena, letting her know without words what they had to do. "We'll get you cleaned up and see what we can do about this Mister Kolar once you're comfortable."

4
———

ALEK MANAGED to get them off the roof, but a group of what looked like construction workers saw them. Nothing he could do about it now but hope that they weren't anti-Alts, even though they were in the area of Cybervid Games, and didn't recognize Octavia. Instead of flying, they took a taxi to keep Octavia comfortable. She was quiet throughout the ride, sniffling a little, with her hands shoved into her pockets.

She directed them up to her apartment complex nearby, a third-floor efficiency with just the basics - a futon covered in a colorful comforter, a kitchenette, and a desktop computer in the corner. The walls were bare, and the desktop looked at least four years old, so probably bought used. Not a bad set-up though, for someone who had bigger expenses to worry about and an unsteady work history.

"Go wash your face." Serena turned her sister toward the bathroom and gave her a gentle shove. "Do you have any coffee or tea?"

"Both," Octavia called back before closing the bathroom door. "Upper cabinet to the right of the sink."

"I got this." Sibling rivalry he could handle— it was easier if it was other people's siblings. He and Evan had their share of arguments, with Nik sometimes getting caught in between. Cory was a pain in the ass because he was the youngest and didn't know when to back off, which led to other problems Alek didn't want to think about right now.

Octavia only had black tea, and he didn't see a coffee maker in the cabinet, so he set water on the stove to boil. The next cupboard over had plenty of mugs, all of them from different sets. He selected three and set them on the stained but clean Formica counter. Serena slipped her hands around his waist from behind, her forehead leaning against his back.

"I don't know what to do with her." Serena's warm hands rubbed his stomach. "She's become my worst nightmare."

If Serena's hands kept going like they were, Octavia wasn't the one who was going to be in trouble. Alek placed his hands on Serena's, holding them in place.

"One problem at a time. Let's get her story first. The real story, not the emotional output. We need to find a way to separate her from Kolar, with a job that will work for her. Then we'll figure out what to do with Kolar."

Octavia came out of the bathroom, still patting her face with a hand towel. Serena removed her arms from around his waist. Octavia frowned but didn't say anything. She headed back into the main room and sat on the futon.

Serena joined her. Even though Octavia tried to keep her voice quiet, Alek could hear her say, "*The Sizzler* said you were marrying the other one? The dark-haired brother with the blue eyes."

"Yeah, I thought so too," Serena responded. "He's moved on and so have I. The rags haven't figured it out yet and we'd like to keep it that way."

"Yeah, okay. This one's got a twin though, right? Maybe you could introduce us?"

The teapot started to whistle so he didn't hear Serena's response. He found it interesting how Octavia's anti-Alt stance shifted with her interest in Evan. After he had set the tea to steep, he generated an air pillow to levitate the three cups and a sugar jar into the main room. There was a plastic dinner tray leaning against the wall. Octavia open it next to the futon, so it stood between where she sat near the pillows and where Serena had curled up near the knitted afghan folded at the foot. Alek pulled over the computer chair for himself.

"Nice trick," Octavia commented, as she watched Serena pour a teaspoon of sugar into her cup.

"You could probably do it too, if you tried."

He could see the instant denial form on Octavia's lips, but then something else kicked in. Her brow smoothed and she licked her lips. "Yeah, maybe. I'll give it a try."

"Not here." Serena passed the sugar to her sister. "And not with hot water. Best wait until we get you to the Arena. It's safer in case something goes wrong."

Octavia made a soft mew of protest but said nothing else. Alek debated his tea. He preferred coffee, so he had no idea about how much sugar to add. He decided following Serena's example was best, so he used his control over the air to levitate the spoon into and out of the jar.

"Show off." The insult from Serena was laced with affection, so Alek grinned.

"That's the catch." Alek decided he'd made his point, so he picked the mug up with his hands. "I've been practicing since I was two years old. My grandfather was like Mister Kolar — he wanted to use our abilities for his own benefit, not for the greater good. He would alternatively bribe us to do his bidding or sic us against one another to push us to our limits. He also trained us like soldiers to fight against the Norms when the Norms rose up against us. He wanted us to protect Blackwood

Enterprises so that he'd have enough money for himself when the Norm revolution happened.

"My mom rejected all of that and kicked him out of the house and out of the company. Mom's Alt ability made it impossible for him to fight back. We haven't seen him in over a decade and — well, you know who my mom is."

"Captain Spectacular, you mean."

"Yeah, but to me she's just 'Mom.' Mother first, Captain second, CEO last, but don't tell the Board of Directors that."

Octavia grinned, but turned her eyes down as he winked. He didn't look at Serena to see what her reaction was. Knowing her, she was internally rolling her eyes at his flirting.

"Tell us more about Mister Kolar. What made you change your mind about him?" Serena crossed her long legs, trying to get comfortable.

"I haven't really changed my mind about him. Like I said, he's the only one who gave me a chance, and thanks to him, I've had a stable life for the past two years. I'm happy working there. I'm happy living here. I wouldn't jeopardize that if I could control this." Octavia wiggled her fingers in the air, which had stopped producing smoke.

"You do know that he'll never accept you if he finds out you're an Alt, right?" Serena sipped her tea. "He can't fire you without drawing attention, but there are other ways of getting people to quit."

"Trust me, I know all about that." Octavia fiddled with the mug. "My previous bosses were experts at getting people they hated to quit."

"So what else happened when you first noticed your Alt power had reactivated?"

Octavia started to bring the mug to her lips, but changed her mind, as if she couldn't enjoy it. "It was around the same time you guys found the quarry prison. I don't know why I started paying attention to that. I usually don't care about what happens in the news. It's all boring stuff, most of the time. Stuff that doesn't affect me."

"You were happy and content." Alek wanted to show her the logic of why she was doing what she was doing. It wasn't just a random whim on her part. He got the impression no one had ever told her she was smart, not even Serena. Someone had to. "You had the time to pay attention, instead of worrying about where you were going to live, where your next meal was coming from."

"That's it, exactly! Everything was going smoothly in my life. I had a job I loved, my own apartment, friends I could count on, and my medication was keeping me stable. I'd never had that before. I never *felt* like that before. Then suddenly T-CASS goes and invades Star Haven and something tripped in my brain, and out of nowhere I remembered when I was seven and had smoke coming out of my fingers!"

The urge to defend T-CASS against the invasion remark parked itself at his lips. Now wasn't the time to get into the details about the quarry raid. Serena's hand found its way to his thigh and he knew she was fighting the same instinct.

"So, I'm watching the news and remembering the smoke, and I think 'that could have been me. I could have been one of Mayor Dane's experiments.' I mean, I was homeless for a while and I have a mental illness, and Mayor Dane preyed on those types of people, right?"

She needed validation that she understood what she'd heard on TV, but she looked to him, not to Serena. "Yes," he said, "you're right. That's exactly what Mayor Dane did."

"I couldn't stop working, though. I mean, I still had bills and rent to pay. So, I just kept going to work like I always did, recruiting new members to join us at the next party. I'm really good at it. I have the highest level of recruitment of all the club members."

She sounded so proud that Alek just let her talk.

"I never thought the smoke would appear again. I'm twenty now, but there I was, sitting in front of my station, and I look down and poof — there's smoke pouring out of my fingers. After thirteen years of nothing. That's a heck of a long time in between. I thought to myself 'no one has to know,' but I couldn't stop it. I went into the bathroom and I soaked my hands like I did when I was a kid, and it went away again. It didn't come back until now." She waved her fingers, which still had smoke wisping out of the tips.

"I suppose I would have left Mister Kolar's on my own, but he said something that really kind of freaked me out."

"What was that?" he asked.

"I was still in the bathroom because the smoke got so bad, I couldn't hide it by shoving my hands into my pockets. He knocked on the door and asked if I was all right. He does that a lot because he really cares about his employees. Anyway, I told him I had cramps and needed a few minutes for the painkillers to work. Perfectly normal stuff, right? But then he asked me if the painkillers would interfere with my Bupropion. I didn't think too much about it at first, but I never told him I was on Bupropion. I mean, he knows I'm on an anti-depressant, and that I need to see my doctor at least once a month, sometimes more if the medication needs adjusting. That's why I couldn't keep a job before now, and I was really honest about it all up front because he seemed like the kind of guy who understood that normal people aren't perfect. He said that, in fact — Norms aren't perfect, and we need to have the right to be imperfect, without living in fear of Alts expecting us to have perfect lives.

"But I couldn't figure out how he knew I was on Bupropion because it's not the same medication I was on two years ago. We changed it to a generic that works just as well but is cheaper so I could save some money. I never told him that. There was no reason for him to know the details, as long as I was stable and doing my job, so how would he know I was on Bupropion?"

Cold silence settled over the room. Alek looked at Serena. From the look on her face, she was thinking the same thing he was: the situation wasn't just about an anti-Alt recruiter anymore.

"He would have to have access to your records," Alek said.

"Yeah, that's what I thought." The excitement in Octavia's voice when she talked about her job disappeared, and her voice dropped to a near whisper. "What kind of employer would have access to my medical records?"

This time Serena answered. "Not a trustworthy one."

Octavia looked as if someone had stolen her teddy bear. Serena reached over to place a hand on Octavia's thigh, careful not to touch her skin. "We'll work through this. If Kolar has illegal access to your records, we'll have him arrested."

Octavia buried her face in her hands. "I'll lose my job."

"We'll find you another one." Serena finished her tea, her word definitive. "A job you can enjoy just as much as this one."

"Everyone will hate me."

Serena didn't seem inclined to respond to that accusation. Too much history with Octavia, he guessed, so Alek answered instead. "You'll make new friends. Friends who don't care if you're an Alt or not. If not being an Alt is a condition of their friendship, they're not your friends."

"I need to think about this."

They were losing her. All of this, and she wasn't even sure if she wanted to leave a man who would prefer to see her dead because of what she could do. So much potential, and the anti-Alts couldn't see it, any of it.

"Why don't you come to my place," Alek suggested.

"Someplace neutral. Someplace safe where Kolar can't track you down."

"Why would he do that?" Octavia frowned. "He doesn't know anything. He thinks I'm a loyal employee. I'm still loyal, sort of."

"He knows your last name." Alek made a pointed look at Serena, so she would know his invitation wasn't just some whim. "It's the same as Serena's. He knows she is an Alt. I think you were targeted. Kolar isn't your friend and he doesn't give a damn about you. He selected you because of Serena. She's his real target and we need to find out what his plans are. We need to do it tonight."

"WHY DIDN'T I CONSIDER THAT?" Serena could have slapped herself senseless.

"You were too close to the problem," Alek said.

God, she couldn't even look at him, her embarrassment was so great. Here, she thought she was ready to take a leading role in T-CASS, and she couldn't even see a trap laid out bare before her.

Alek reached for her hand, a gesture of comfort she accepted. "You were concerned only for your sister, so the bigger picture slipped by."

Octavia looked from Alek to Serena and back again. "You're saying I don't even play a leading role in my own super villain plot? I'm not even the sidekick or the perky companion? I'm just the bait?"

Ouch. The pain in Octavia's voice hurt all way across the bed. Serena didn't know what to say to the sister who had forever lived in her shadow. Serena had to scramble to come up with something comforting to say. "What you are is the key to putting a stop to this before someone gets hurt."

At least Alek had the grace to nod in agreement. "Right, the key."

"The key, how?"

"I think we should talk about this later." Octavia never did know when to let go of a conversation alone. "If Alek is right and I'm really the target, I think we should bypass his place and head to T-CASS HQ. That's the safest place in the city for an untrained Alt. There's no way Kolar will be able to get his hands on you while you're there."

"I don't know...."

"Octavia, please, just trust me for once." Serena desperately wanted to reach out and take her sister's hands into hers. How she wished she had brought a pair of gloves with her, so she could safely do just that. "I know there's a lot for you to process here. I know you're hurting because you feel as if you're giving up a good situation that has sustained you for two years, but I need you to understand, it's not just your life that's in jeopardy. The anti-Alts are getting stronger and more deadly. Even if you can hide your ability from Kolar, even if he's not smart enough to figure out that we're related, even if he's really a pacifist who won't hurt anyone even as he preaches his intolerance for Alts, you cannot trust those around him. All it takes is one person to betray you, and you'll find yourself dead, or worse. Hell, someone might even kill Kolar for hiring you in the first place."

Octavia's eyes widened. At least now Serena knew her sister understood the stakes.

Alek stood up. "If we're going to go, let's do it now. We'll launch from the roof and head straight up, beyond where anyone on the ground can see us."

Octavia scrambled off the futon. "Won't people see us take off?"

"One of us will create a distraction down on the street." Alek was already heading for the door. "Something harmless that'll draw everyone's attention to ground level."

"Bring a jacket." Serena reached for the nearby hamper with clean clothes in it. Two layers down, she found a light button-down sweater. Too light for an extended flight but it was better than nothing. "It'll be colder higher up in the atmosphere. We'll get you new clothes later."

"Wait. Grab my medication off the kitchen counter." Octavia reached behind a pillow and pulled out a doll. *Cici.* Serena recognized it even though it had seen better days.

Serena held Cici while Octavia bundled up. When Octavia finished with the buttons, Alek ushered them into the hallway. Now that her upper body was covered, Serena could put her arms around her sister's shoulders. At least Octavia didn't pull away.

Their footsteps echoed on the concrete steps heading up to the roof. The maintenance door was unlocked. Alek held it open, motioning Serena through first, then Octavia.

The second her feet hit the roof, she knew the trap was sprung, but she was too late. Underneath her, a thin net stretched from the end of the door to the nearest air conditioning vent. From above, another net dropped.

The electro-shock snapped. Behind her, Octavia screamed. Serena fell flat. The last thing she saw was Cici lying on the roof, blood smeared across the doll's face.

When Serena opened her eyes she was surrounded by pure black. Nothing moved, but she could hear sounds in a vague muffled way. Footsteps, maybe? Her head pounded in a rhythm out of sync with her heart. At least she had a heartbeat, so that was something.

Tight flexicuffs kept her wrists behind her back, so she decided to deal with those in a minute. Despite the headache she lifted her head, leaning forward to explore the area surrounding her. Soft fuzzy curls tickled her nose. Octavia's hair.

"Tavia," she whispered. "Can you hear me?"

A soft moan responded, followed by incoherent mumbling. Octavia was alive, but not fully awake yet. Serena rolled in the other direction, hoping beyond hope she would roll into...

"Stop. Don't touch."

She almost cried at hearing Alek's voice. "They were waiting for us. This must have been their plan since they recruited her two years ago. Wait for Tavia to contact me and draw me to her, then use her against us."

No response. Bastards must have hurt Alek in some way. The room had no light for her to draw on for manipulation. Who knew what they had done to incapacitate Alek?

"Agreed," he finally said, his voice sounding rusty.

"I'll get us out of here, Alek. I swear I will."

More harsh breathing from his direction, so she didn't say anything more. Instead, she worked on digging her bound feet into the floor, in order to shove herself in a third direction. If she could find a wall, she could trace it to whatever door their captors had used to toss them all in here. A door would lead to another room, and maybe a light source. Just one sliver of light was all she needed.

"Guns."

Alek again. What had they done to him?

"Okay, they have guns," she said. "Good to know. Just be still. I'm looking for the door." Her head thumped against a wall as she spoke. Pain exploded behind her eyes.

Kolar had better have left the premises because she planned to kill him.

"Fucked up."

"No, Alek, you didn't fuck up. We all walked into the trap."

"He didn't walk into the trap." Octavia moaned again, but her voice was clear. "He never made it outside, so they missed him. He fought them. Would have won, but the men were going to kill me. They had a gun pressed to my head. Alek surrendered to save me. He told them I wasn't an Alt, and to let me go free because anti-Alts aren't supposed to kill Norms. The men said they'd ask Mister Kolar first. They tied me up and hit me on the head."

"Thanks for telling me, Tavia." Serena kept moving along the wall, using her head to feel for anything that felt like a seam, which could be the location of a door. "Be still, Alek. I'm going to try and contact Pathia."

Another ragged breath. "On leave."

Of course Pathia would follow orders like the rest of them. The telepath wouldn't be listening for emergencies. As much as everyone would like to think she could monitor the entire city 24/7, she had the ability to shut down her telepathy so she could rest.

"I'll try Looper." Looper was a low-level telepath who worked as a Neutral, an Alt who freelanced her abilities instead of working for T-CASS. She claimed she could only loop memories, not hear them from across the city. Still, it was better than nothing.

"Fucked up."

"Stop it, Alek. You didn't..."

"Not me. Them."

Serena stopped her crawl across the floor. "How do you mean, them?"

Another sharp breath. He was fighting whatever it was that kept him immobile. "Wrapped in live electric wire. Trap for Nik, not me."

Nik could travel through solid matter, but he had to avoid live wires while doing it. Kolar must have paid attention to the news and assumed she was still dating Nik, not Alek.

"Still can use ability."

Alek could manipulate the air molecules to help them get free, as long as he could withstand the electrical shock from the net and stay conscious. Serena started moving again, another three feet or so. A sharp edge pricked the skin on her forehead.

"I found the edge to the door, I think." She pressed herself flat, but even between the floor and the door, there was no light. "They must have fortified the bottom of the door with material to prevent light from escaping."

Heavy footsteps pounded outside the door. Serena rolled away in case the guards decided to open it. A minute passed, then two, but no one came through the door.

"What are they waiting for?" Octavia asked.

"Depends on what their plan is. They probably don't want to kill us in Thunder City. It's safer for them to deal with us somewhere else and leave no evidence for anyone to find. With most of T-CASS off duty, they have a better chance of succeeding." Serena swung herself up to a sitting position as best she could. "If there's light on the other side of the door, they won't risk opening it and activating my power."

"Wait, you were at the quarry raid. How did you use your power then?" It sounded as if Octavia was trying to sit up like Serena had.

"I usually create light spheres, or my light slide, ahead of time to draw from. Don't forget the moon, plus the quarry itself had outside lights once you got close enough. Not to mention the lightning generated by Roar and Rumble. I don't need much to create with, just a little is enough."

"What do we do now?" Octavia asked.

Good question. "It would help if we knew where we were."

"We have to be at Cybervid."

"How do you know?"

Octavia took a deep breath. " I can smell curry. And fish. A couple of my frie... former colleagues like a frozen food curry with fish that you can get across the street. They microwave it all the time. Stinks up the place."

"That helps a lot. Good job, Octavia."

"Smoke." That was from Alek.

"You smell smoke?"

More slow breathing. It sounded less labored and more like a carefully controlled rhythm. "No. Push smoke under the door. Set off fire...alarm... sprinklers."

She waited in case he stopped to get his breath back before continuing. There had to be more, because Alek knew as well as she did that even if the alarm triggered a response from the fire department, Kolar would just meet them outside and say it was a false alarm.

"Create convection. Create lightning."

Oh shit. She had a vague idea of how Alek's ability worked. To generate lightning, he needed moisture to both heat and cool to develop a convection. To the best of her memory, he'd never done it inside a building before. Always outside, particularly when there were clouds above.

"Wait. He wants *me* to create smoke?"

"You can do it, Tavia. I know you can. Head toward my voice."

The buttons from her sister's sweater scraped across the floor, so Serena knew she was doing as she was told.

"Now, get down low. Can you feel where the door is?"

"Um, yes, I think so."

"You need to turn around, so your back is to the door, and push your fingers close to the crack. You want to aim as much smoke outside as you can. If we get too much smoke in here, we could suffocate."

"But my ability just happens without me thinking about it."

"No, you activated your ability both times. You don't know yet what the trigger is." Good Lord, it sometimes took an Alt weeks or months to learn how to control their ability. She didn't have that kind of time. "Do you remember what you were thinking about when you first saw your fingers generating smoke?"

"I was angry at you." Octavia's voice was quiet with guilt. "I was seven when you were accepted into T-CASS's training program, the youngest Alt ever. The news made a big deal about you. Your face was everywhere, and I couldn't escape. All Dad wanted to talk about was you and your ability, and how proud he was of you. He never wanted to talk about me. Then you were there on the news again for the quarry raid and the harbor attack. You're everywhere, on the TV, on the internet, in the newspapers. I can't escape."

"Well, that's just something you're going to have to get used to." Serena didn't have time to train Octavia the right way, so brute force would have to do the trick. She flopped onto her back and guessed at where her sister's hands were, then shoved her feet between the door and her sister's back to pin Octavia's hands in place. "I'm older and I'll always be older, and as your older sister, I'll always be better. I'm smarter, faster, and stronger than you because I spent my life training instead running away. I've dedicated my life to helping people, not hurting them. You want to know why our father always talked about me and not you — it's because you never did anything worth bragging about."

"You bitch!" Octavia seethed. She tried to pull her hands away, but Serena kept her feet stomped on the wriggling hands, so Octavia couldn't move them away from the door.

"You think you're the first person to call me a bitch? Half my trainees won't speak to me unless they're ordered to because I push them, and push them, and push them, until they can activate their abilities on command and wield them as ordered. I don't push anyone harder than I push myself. If you think I'm going to let you die in this damn closet, in the dark, where you can't even see my face when you insult me, you had better think again, little sister."

"*I hate you! I hate you! I hate you! I hate you! I hate you...*'

Serena caught a whiff of smoke, which could mean that her sister was still only producing minute amounts that did them no good, or that in her anger she was generating a lot more and pushing it through the infinitesimal crack between the floor and the door, past the material hiding the light from outside. If there was even light outside.

Her sister's voice cracked as she screamed out her hatred. Serena prayed for a signal that their plan worked before she started prodding Octavia again. She didn't want to, but if it meant saving their lives, then Octavia's hatred was worth it.

Another minute passed. Octavia's anger wound down to heaving sobs. Serena thought she had failed when above her head, the water sprinklers hissed before pouring water onto them.

"Get away from the door," Alek yelled.

Serena released her sister's hands. "You did it, Octavia. You did it."

Before Octavia could respond, a thunderous clap pounded against the room. Across the ceiling, forked lightning spread around the door and beyond. Serena thought she heard screams. Footsteps echoed around them. The electronic lock on the door clicked, then opened. Light poured through the small crack into the storeroom.

"Stay still."

Wet hands encircled hers. "Alek, how'd you get free?"

"I'll explain later. Let me get the cuffs off of you. My hands are slippery, so this might dig into your skin."

Did it ever, but in the end, the flexicuffs snapped under the air forced between her skin and the cuffs. The sensation of sharp blood restriction was nothing compared to the freedom of movement for her hands and feet. Octavia still looked like she wanted to deck Serena, but she held her peace while Alek freed her, too.

Serena stood to keep watch out the door. All the computer equipment in the storeroom looked fried beyond repair. Dark scorch marks decorated the walls from the lightning Alek had called down. Even the microwave zapped under the sprinklers still pouring water from overhead.

"C'mon, let's get out of here." Alek tossed the broken cuffs into a corner.

Serena let Alek guide Octavia, his arm secured around her sister's shoulders. They stomped through the water on the floor toward front entrance. Outside, all of the Cybervid Games employees huddled around the entrance looking confused, not knowing where to go or what to do next.

"Where's Kolar?" Serena shouted at them. "Where is he?"

No one answered her. They knew who she was, and what she was. As a group, they stared at Octavia, killing her with their thoughts.

Serena had no time for their hate, but she would make time for her own anger. She formed a light sphere bigger than a basketball, then another, then another. "I'm going to start lobbing these at your heads if I don't get an answer now! Where the fuck is Kolar?"

"He left," a sandy-haired girl to her left said. Those around the girl tried to shush her.

She fought back. "Shut up. Kolar ditched us. I'm not going to get my brains splattered on the sidewalk for him." She turned back to Serena. "He took off. He parks in the public lot around the corner. He said we should go home too, but most of us take the bus, and we know we can't outrun you."

"Damn right, you can't." Serena dissipated the spheres. "What car does he drive?"

"Mercedes. Silver. Four doors. I don't know the year."

Serena dissipated the spheres and created a light slide large enough to hold three people. "You better hope Roar's lightning fried Kolar's payroll records too, or you're going to have the cops on your doorstep before tomorrow morning."

Alek helped Octavia stand on the light slide. Serena ignored their skin touching. At this point, they had bigger problems. "Hang on to me," she told her sister. "We're going hunting."

With a thought, she propelled the slide forward and up, heading for the parking lot. Octavia gripped Serena's soaked shirt, while Alek sandwiched her in between the two of them. The parking lot was half full, but they saw no sign of a silver car.

"Higher. We need to see all of the side streets," Alek said.

"Oooo, look who's getting bossy," Serena shouted back. She was in her element — flying high, serving justice. Some days, training others just didn't cut it.

"I see him. I see him." Octavia pointed over her shoulder to the northwest. "It's a silver four-door."

"Let's check it out." Serena swooped down, pacing the car but trying to stay in its blind spot.

"Are you sure it's him?" She could barely hear Alek above the wind. "We're still too high to look in the window."

"He has a *Battleguards* bumper sticker," Octavia confirmed.

"We're going to have to get lower. He might see us." Serena didn't like those odds.

"If it's not him, it won't matter," Alek said. "If it is him, we'll blow out his back tires."

Serena pulled in behind the car, but in front of the pickup truck following. She saw the familiar *Battleguards* logo, clear as day. Kolar saw them too, as he sped up.

"Oh, no, you don't." Before Alek could hit the tires with his own power, Serena formed two light spheres, but this time with spikes. She tossed them with precision at the same time. Both back tires popped, dragging the car to an undramatic ending.

Alek used his wind vortex to lift the car before it slowed down traffic, then propped it up on the shoulder.

"Hold tight, Tavia." Serena already knew what she had to do to finish the job. "The slide is going to disappear. Be prepared to drop."

Octavia did, and the three of them landed on the street next to the car. Kolar got out, but at least did them the courtesy of not running. He was done and he knew it.

"Where's our comms?" Alek left Octavia's side to confront Kolar, hulking over the man. There wasn't that much of a height difference, but Alek had the body of a weightlifter. Next to him, the older man didn't stand a chance.

"In the trunk." Kolar pulled off his glasses off with a sigh and wiped them down with a handkerchief.

Alek backed away from Kolar. The second he did, Octavia charged past Alek with a shriek of rage and body slammed Kolar against the car. "How could you? I would have done anything for you! I hate you!"

Serena watched Kolar's eyes bulge as Octavia slapped her hands over the lower half of his face. Serena stepped forward to pull her sister off the man before he struck her back.

"No, wait." Alek put a hand on Serena's shoulder. "Give her a second."

Serena could now see what Alek saw. Smoke poured out of Octavia's hands into Kolar's nose and down his throat. He gagged, trying to strike back, but Octavia didn't let up. He started to choke.

"Okay, *now* we can stop her."

Alek let Serena do the honors of hauling her sister away

from the near unconscious man, while Alek prevented him from falling.

"It's okay, Tavia. I got you. You're going to be okay." For the first time ever, Serena rocked her little sister as Octavia cried in her arms.

ALEK KEPT his phone report to T-CASS brief. He and Serena had been involved in an incident near Bolton Park. The police had taken their statements and were handling it. The worker bee handling his call told him to hold for a moment.

"I have a message from the Captain."

Not unusual, Alek thought, so he waited.

"She says you are to report home no later than eight o'clock tomorrow morning. Earlier is better."

Home meant the Blackwood Estate where he'd grown up. Not a problem; he usually tried to get over there once a month for a visit, anyway. Except this time, he'd ask Serena if she'd join him. Would she though, knowing Nik would more than likely be there?

Only one way to find out, but he waited until the three of them were back at his apartment. Luckily for Octavia, not only were their comms in the trunk, but so were her medication and her doll, Cici. He promised to arrange for the doll to be cleaned of blood. As soon as she got her training schedule, he also would make sure that everything remaining in her apartment was ready to move to a new apartment closer to the Arena.

"Here you go." He opened the door to the second bedroom. "It's a little sparse furniture-wise, but..."

"It's huge."

He could hear Serena sniggering in the hallway. "Well, I guess. You'll at least be comfortable. There's going to be more police reports, and possibly a trial. While you're here, you won't have to worry about Kolar's people coming after you."

"Will they all be arrested? Will I..."

"I'm not a lawyer or a police officer, but you really didn't do anything wrong." Alek turned on the bathroom lights, so she could explore her new space in full. "If all you did was invite people to parties, then I can't see why they would arrest you."

She nodded, but her eyes were already closing, so he motioned her farther into the room and closed the door behind her.

Serena pulled him into a hug before he could go any further. "Thank you. Now that we've been through all of this, I don't want to let her out of my sight, or at least not out of my range."

"My home is yours, and as long as it's yours, it's also hers." He ran his hands up and down her back. Having her in his arms gave him strength, which he needed right now. Going to bed, even with Serena, filled him with a certain dread. What if his memory loops led to nightmares? If he started thrashing about, he could hurt Serena.

She pulled back; her eyes also tired.

"Do you want to sleep alone tonight?" he asked. "I could take the couch, and you wouldn't have to worry about me ravishing you in the middle of the night."

"Ravishing me? Sounds like the best proposition I've had all day, possibly all week." Her eyes drooped again, though. "I am sleepy, but I want to sleep in your bed with you by my side, at least for tonight. I know T-CASS schedules are crazy, but if I ever feel as if I need a night on my own, I'll just go back to my apartment, which I'm keeping for now."

He nodded. He couldn't blame her. She still would have to see Nik regularly, and he couldn't imagine having to work with your ex and not needing some space at the start of a new relationship.

"Before we hit the sack though, I want to talk to you about those headaches of yours."

Just the mention of his headaches threatened to start the loop again. He tried to push it away, but the image was there, fighting back at his attempt.

"If we're going to talk about that, let's go back to the living room. I'm going to need to sit down for this."

A frown marred Serena's sleepy features, but she followed him back into the living room. Back to the sofa where all of this had started. Hell, *Battleguards* was still active on the screen. He shoved all the equipment aside so he could sit close to Serena. Thank the love gods that she cuddled right up next to him and took his free hand.

"The headaches aren't really headaches." No point in wasting time on frivolous niceties. "They're nightmares, except I don't have to be asleep to have them."

"About the harbor? About Evan?" She looked at him now, her gorgeous brown eyes wide with sorrow.

"About you."

"Me?"

"Serena, you flew your light slide under the cargo container we were carrying."

She didn't get it. "Of course. I had to get the Star Haven delegates out from under there in case you couldn't hold the container."

"I had to make a choice, Serena. I had to choose between dropping the container on you and saving Evan, or letting Evan fall into the fire to save you. I chose you."

"I... I don't...I can't..." She stopped and started again. "You did the right thing. Not because of me; because of the others."

"I know I did the right thing. *Now*. It doesn't make it better." He pushed away from her so he could face her. "Evan fell into an inferno. For all I knew at the time, he was unconscious and burning alive in there. I couldn't see the ground. I didn't know if you had gotten out from under me. The container knocked into my leg and broke it because I couldn't get it stable fast enough. So I'm hanging there with a broken leg, and I've just watched my brother die. The fact that he didn't die doesn't make it any better. The fact that Cory had to hold my hand in the hospital so I wouldn't kill any of the doctors because I was out of my head with grief doesn't make it better.

"I let my brother fall because I cared more about you than I did about him, and I don't know what to do about that. I don't know if I could make that decision again."

Serena pulled her legs up so she could sit crossed legged, and she took his hands. "I can't promise you that you won't ever have to make that kind of decision again. Evan knows that, and you have to talk to him about it. You made a decision today to surrender to a man who could have killed all of us."

"That was different. Kolar's plan was flawed — "

"I don't care how flawed it was; we still could have died if he'd been one of the hard-core anti-Alts who attacked the harbor. *They* would have shot us dead when we were unconscious. *You* made a choice, and I accept that choice. You chose me and the delegates over your brother, knowing T-CASS would not abandon him. Don't make me your excuse for foolish choices, Alek. Don't make the harbor attack an excuse for a relationship with me."

"Is that what you think this is?" Alek pulled away from her. "I told you — "

"Yes, I know. You've had a crush on me since you were thirteen because I gave you the best present ever."

"It's not just that."

"It better not be, because I can't do this if you're going to change who you are for me."

What was she talking about? "I wouldn't."

"Good. Because I'm in love with you too, Alek. I didn't think it would hit me this fast, but we worked well together today. We've always worked well together. When everyone else treats me like the mean old drill sergeant, and doesn't invite me to their parties or for a drink after work or even to the club for a round of tennis or whatever, I get it. I'm not someone they want to be around because they think what they see at work is what I am all the time. You never treat me as if I'm going to crap on everyone else's fun, and we don't necessarily have to be with other people to enjoy ourselves. You're just better at faking it than I am. I can have fun too, and I'd like it if we could have fun together."

"Wait, you just said you loved me."

"Yes, I did."

"I love you, too." He meant it. Those words he'd been wanting to say to her, he finally could say to her with his whole heart.

"Well good, because I didn't want to give up eleven and a half inches because you don't love me."

"Now, that's just a rumor I read in the paper. I haven't actually measured myself."

Serena raised a single dark eyebrow.

"I haven't. I swear."

"Then we'll just leave it as a mystery." There was still some cider in the bottle left on the coffee table. She grabbed it and swallowed it down, before setting the bottle down again. "I still expect you to see a doctor. How you chose to deal with your nightmares or memory loops is up to you. I will support you however you choose to deal with it, but you *will* deal with it. You won't shove it aside and pretend it doesn't affect both of us."

He took his now-empty bottle and placed it back on the table so he could hold her hands in his. "I swear to you, Serena. I will talk to Evan, and I will see a doctor. I will make this right for both of us because I want you in my life forever."

She kissed him, her lips dancing across his in ways he'd only imagined before, pulling away just long enough to issue one more order. "Take me to your bedroom, Blackwood. If you're going to love me forever, I want you to start right now."

***

IF YOU ENJOYED A SECRET LOVE check out the most recent adventure featuring the Blackwood brothers, A SECRET LIFE. Keep reading for a sneak peek.

He scorches the earth with lightning. She creates maelstroms from the bottom of the sea. When dark and light clash over a clandestine terrorist investigation, will the fallout destroy their only chance at love?

WORD OF MOUTH and reviews are vital for any author to succeed. If you enjoyed BLOOD SURFER, please consider leaving a review. A simple sentence or two sharing your thoughts about the book would be helpful to other readers. Thank you!

Chapter One

DURING THE GRAND finale of Blood Hunter.

"GET DOWN. YOU KNOW BETTER." Evan Blackwood had to take his hand off the electric can opener to remove the offended feline from the kitchen counter. He could have used his Alt power to lift the cat off, but animals in general didn't react well to his ability to manipulate air molecules. The three beasts acted as if they hadn't been fed in days. In reality, he had fed his menagerie before dawn because he hadn't slept well and needed the distraction. The cats didn't care. He hadn't been home for most of the past two weeks, abandoning them, as far as they were concerned. When he had finally fallen asleep, the nightmare resumed, tossing and turning him until he woke again a few minutes ago.

The cats hadn't cared about his nightmares either. They demanded a second breakfast by pouncing on his chest. The older tom even had the audacity to dig a claw into Evan's nose, which forced him out from under the sweat-soaked sheets. Further retribution would be forthcoming.

The premium wet stuff filled three individual bowls, which Evan placed on the floor, two of them together at one end of the kitchen and the third at the opposite end. If he placed all three together, the two older bullies would eat the food of the youngest. Then he cleaned the counter before pulling out fish food for his aquariums, followed by pellets for his gerbils. He hadn't planned on keeping the gerbils. The animal rescue group he worked with had found a dozen of them in a home the police raided and had nowhere else to place them. There weren't many takers for gerbils, but the rescue group had sworn up, down, and sideways to keep trying to find them a forever home.

In the background, the television droned. The white noise kept him focused on his chores, and off himself. He didn't want to think about himself. He didn't want to remember...

He dropped the bag of gerbil pellets and jammed the palms of his hands into his eyes as the memory loop started again.

He couldn't see the explosion because his back was toward the ship. He'd been generating an air pillow with his brother, but the scorching heat seared his body. In front of him, Alek's face switched from casual focus to absolute horror. The cargo container they balanced in mid-air started to slip. Evan no sooner registered what had gone wrong when metal debris slammed into him. The impact damn near knocked him unconscious. His Alt ability wavered even more, unable to keep hold of the container.

White light behind his eyes obscured his vision. He could no longer see Alek, but he could hear Alek scream his name. His brother's voice faded as he fell, the heat intensifying as he hit the deck. Flames roared around him, licking his uniform, then his skin. By instinct alone, Evan ignored his broken bones and shoved away the air molecules surrounding him.

Starving the fire of oxygen meant he had almost no air to breathe. With his eyes closed against the heat, he couldn't tell how far back he'd pushed the fire. He could only lie there, gulping what few super heated molecules had slipped past his barrier with his failing strength, hoping his teammates would rescue him before he lost consciousness.

He didn't actually remember his rescue. The power he exerted to keep himself alive made him blind to everything else. At some point his mother, still wet from keeping the cargo ship afloat, pulled him above the firestorm before flying him home instead of to the hospital.

He had known she was going to ask Hannah Quinn to heal him, but the charred skin on his face made it impossible to talk. Captain Spectacular had almost lost two sons — Nik and Cory — in the past two weeks. In the end, he couldn't blame her for ignoring protocol, and her own directive, by asking Hannah to do the one thing the bloodsurfer wasn't supposed to do.

Whether the Oversight Committee and the people of Thunder City agreed with his mother's decision was another problem for another day.

A loud chime jolted him out of the nightmare. He pulled his comm from its clip on his jeans with sweat soaked hands. Messages for Thunder City's Alt Support Services, T-CASS, poured across the screen in rapid succession as the teams assembled.

A bomb threat had been called in. The target: Harbor Regional Hospital. The operations manager demanded silence during the evacuation. No sirens, no flashing lights. A final message sank his heart: his stepfather, Thomas Carraro, had been shot.

Evan scrolled faster. No orders for him, though, and no orders for Alek. Both he and his brother were grounded since everyone believed they were still recovering from the harbor attack. Evan checked his phone for personal messages. Nothing yet. His mother would be in the thick of the evacuation, and his eldest brother, Nik, knew how to deactivate bombs. He wouldn't hear from them until the threat was over.

Along with his family, the usual team members responded: Blockhead, Mach Ten, Flame, Spritz...Evan couldn't help but notice that Gilly hadn't responded. Headquarters more than likely hadn't summoned her. Their loss. Like Spritz, Gilly could control water molecules. Unlike Spritz, Gilly had been born with gills so she could breath under water. She spent most of her time in Mystic Bay or working at the city's aquarium. Despite assisting in saving his life during the harbor attack, no one had thought to summon her to a land-based terrorist attack at the hospital.

Evan's thumb hovered over the comm. Should he remind HQ that Gilly was an important member of the team? That she also had superhuman strength? Would Gilly appreciate him bringing her to the attention of the operations team?

Probably not. Gilly didn't like people too much and he hadn't seen her at HQ in almost a month. Actually, he hadn't realized until now that he'd been looking for her at HQ when he was there.

Evan clamped down on the extra thump from his heart. Now wasn't the time for thinking about a woman, especially a teammate, like that. In the living room, the news reporter on the screen was live downtown. Evan grabbed the fish food and gerbil pellets while he listened to the broadcast.

"...yes, that's all we know at this point. Terrorists have placed bombs all around Harbor Regional Hospital. T-CASS and the police have responded. They are evacuating the hospital as quickly as possible, and all traffic has been detoured. If you are in need of emergency care, here are the alternatives..."

Feeding the fish tugged him away from the temptation to respond despite not receiving orders. Still, the instinct to do something, anything, remained. His comm pinged before that thought went any further and a priority icon popped up. A private message from his mother for him and Alek.

Don't you two even think about it. Stay away. I'll contact you if I need you.

Evan dropped the comm onto the sofa and headed toward his bedroom where he had two more fish tanks, his annoyance at war with the logic of his mother's message. He could only assume that his mother didn't want to advertise the fact that Hannah had broken the law on behalf of the Blackwoods.

There was nothing he could do about it. He didn't dare interrupt his mother during an operation to complain. She would share any information about Thomas when she had time. If Thomas died....

Worrying about something before it happened served no purpose, so Evan headed into the spare bedroom where he had set up the gerbil cages. He knew how much his mother would hurt if Thomas died, and he would support her no matter what.

Unlike Alek, Evan had made peace with Thomas a long time ago.

Finished feeding his pets, Evan returned to the living room and scooped up the calico so he could sit on the sofa while he called his brother. Alek didn't answer on his first attempt, so Evan called again, and he kept calling until Alek finally answered.

"You're not responding to your comm," Evan said.

The background noise ceased, so Alek must have silenced one of his video games. "I woke up a little while ago. We're on medical leave until mom says otherwise. No one should be contacting us via the comm."

"There's been an attack on Harbor Regional Hospital." Evan paused. "Thomas has been shot. Mom is down there with Nik. Someone's planted bombs around the hospital."

Evan waited, hoping Alek wouldn't brush off the shooting because it was Thomas and not one of their teammates.

"I'll be ready in five," Alek said. "You can meet me at the corner of — "

"No way." Evan interrupted his brother's plan, though he was relieved that Alek was ready for action. "We can't go down there. Mom's orders. Check your damn comm."

He waited again while Alek found their mother's message. "All right. We won't go downtown, but we can still go to HQ."

"If you want." Evan knew exactly why Alek wanted to go to HQ. Serena would be working with the Star Haven Newcomers. She was the one person Alek cared for more than their family. He'd have to needle his brother about it another day. "But don't wear your uniform, and use the roof entrance. I think Mom's more worried about advertising our sudden recovery."

"Will you meet me there?" Alek asked.

So he could watch Alek make a fool of himself pursuing Nik's long-time and very ex-fiancée? No way was he going to put himself in the middle of that drama, not even for his twin. "No. I'm going to the clinic. They're short handed as it is."

"Will do." Alek hung up, so Evan clipped his comm and phone to his jeans. He gave the calico a quick scratch behind her ears before heading out to the deck. His apartment overlooked West Ashland Park and was a quick five minute flight to the veterinary practice where he worked part-time.

Adding power to the wind, Evan created a vortex to launch himself toward the sky. He climbed over the top of the apartment building, then banked toward the Bayside neighborhood.

He'd only been flying for a few minutes when a shock wave hit, followed by muffled boom. The wave wasn't powerful enough to knock him off course, but he stopped mid-flight to figure out where it had originated. In the distance, the clouds rippled as smoke billowed out over downtown.

Alek! The university district was closer to Harbor Regional than he was. If Alek had launched at the same time he had...

The scent of sugar cookies filled his nose.

Alek is fine, Evan.

Pathia.

The shock wave only knocked him off course. His first concern was for the Captain, then you.

Evan flashed images of the rest of his family through his mind, a quick way to ask Pathia about their status.

They are all fine, except I cannot find Hannah. I'm not able to read her, but I'm not as familiar with her thoughts as I am with you and your family. An ambulance is transporting Thomas to the Fargrounds Medical Center. I'll keep looking for Hannah, I promise.

Thunder City would riot if Hannah died.

Keep going, Evan. I've got this. If something happens, I'll let you know.

Evan visualized a bouquet of flowers for Pathia. The scent of sugar cookies grew stronger for a second, then disappeared. Evan looked back at the downtown skyline.

The memory loop started again.

Pain.

Flames.

No oxygen.

Dying.

Without focus he lost control of his vortex and tumbled head over heel, barely catching himself before he hit the ground. He had to get out of here, find someplace to escape his thoughts.

From this height, he could just about see the edge of Silvergrass Pier. This time of day there would be a handful of fisherman, but if he settled himself on the boulders shoring up the wooden structure, no one would bother him. It took a supreme amount of focus to get his mind off his family and fly toward the shore.

Mystic Bay reflected the early morning sun along calm waters. As he suspected, there was only one fisherman, and he appeared to be packing up his equipment in a hurry. Maybe he'd heard the explosion? Did he know someone who worked downtown? Evan's fear turned to anger. No one should have to have their lives disrupted at the whims of the hate-mongers.

Still, he now had the entire Pier to himself, so he flew to the point. Instead of lowering himself onto one of the boulders, he hovered in place, his back to both the harbor and the heart of Thunder City.

Over the horizon sat Star Haven, but he could ignore that nasty source of Thunder City's troubles, and just watch the calm waves roll toward the shore. In the distance, a few dolphins leapt out of the water, diving back in without a care in the world. Maybe this was why Gilly spent more time swimming in the Bay rather than with her teammates. Under the water's surface, what could go wrong? It would be cold, but peaceful, and no anti-Alts trying to kill him or his family.

He'd let his imagination wander, finding a little inner peace, until something slammed into his head.

Pain.

Flames.

No oxygen.

Dying.

He fell toward the boulders below.

***

ALSO BY DEBRA JESS

If you like Science Fiction, check out the complete Heroes of
Andromeda series starting with ANDROMEDA'S REBEL:

**They took the sky from her, and her memory, but no one could take
away her rebellious spirit.**

If you prefer Urban Fantasy, DREAM OF MY SOUL is now available.

**A vampire must protect the world's only vampire hunter (who also
happens to be her ex-fiancé) from the demon who hunts both of
them.**

ACKNOWLEDGMENTS

Writing is a tough gig on a good day. When life tosses lemors at you like fastballs and you don't have the sugar to make lemonade, the publishing industry can overwhelm you with negative energy. I've a rough year and my books had to be delayed because of it, but I've also had a tremendous amount of support from my friends, my colleagues, and my readers. Without their support, I might have given up on this publishing dream. Yet, here I am with a new book and another on the way. So, thank you to those who have stuck with me. I see blue skies ahead and many more stories for you to enjoy.

ABOUT THE AUTHOR

A Connecticut Yankee transplanted to Central Florida, Debra Jess writes science fiction romance, science fantasy, superheroes, and urban fantasy. She began writing in 2006, combining her love of fairy tales and Star Wars to craft original stories of ordinary people in extraordinary adventures and fantastical creatures in out-of-this world escapades. Along the way she's acquired a love for stray cats, flower gardens, and traveling for her own adventures. You can follow Debra Jess's adventures by subscribing to her newsletter on her website

Facebook

Instagram

Threads

Bluesky

For the latest information on Debra Jess's book releases, please sign up for her newsletter on her website.

Your email address will never be shared and you can unsubscribe at any time.